EXHIBIT THIS!
THE MUSEUM COMEDIES

by

LUIGI JANNUZZI

SAMUEL FRENCH

FOUNDED 1830

SAMUELFRENCH.COM

IMPORTANT BILLING AND CREDIT REQUIREMENTS

All producers of *EXHIBIT THIS! THE MUSEUM COMEDIES must* give credit to the Author of the Play in all programs distributed in connection with performances of the Play, and in all instances in which the title of the Play appears for the purposes of advertising, publicizing or otherwise exploiting the Play and/or a production. The name of the Author *must* appear on a separate line on which no other name appears, immediately following the title and *must* appear in size of type not less than fifty percent of the size of the title type.

ABOUT THE AUTHOR

#1 Pick of New York Magazine in the Midtown International Play Festival, winner of the Perry Award for the best play in New Jersey Theater and played to spectacular reviews, awards and sold out performances in New York City, *EXHIBIT THIS! – THE MUSEUM COMEDIES* are Luigi Jannuzzi's seventh to nineteenth published plays.

Individually, the plays have won 3 Samuel French Finalist Awards, two Off-Off Broadway Awards (OOBR.com) and have been performed from NYC to London.

Luigi's Website: www.LuigiJannuzzi.com
The Art in the plays are featured there along with the reviews/posters/etc.

The author's other published comedies include:
Full lengths: *NIGHT OF THE FOOLISH MOON*
                FOR THE LOVE OF JULIET
One Acts: *A BENCH AT THE EDGE*
                THE APPOINTMENT
                THE BARBARIANS ARE COMING
                WITH OR WITHOUT YOU.

Luigi's play *A BENCH AT THE EDGE* won best one act in Ireland in 1999 and best one act in Scotland and The United Kingdom in 2001. He is a recipient of two New Jersey State Council on the Arts Fellowships, two Geraldine R. Dodge Grants, three National Endowments for the Humanities (2000 at Rutgers U., 1998 at Columbia U., and 1995 at The U Of Vermont) the 1986 Goshen Peace Prize, a 2000 and 1998 Finalist in the Eugene O"Neill National Playwriting conference, and is a 2007 – 2009 James Madison seminar participant at Princeton University.

He is a member of the Dramatist Guild, Author's Guild, NJTEC, NJ REP, the Metropolitan Theatre Company, and NJDramatist/Waterfront Ensemble. Mr. Jannuzzi born in Bound Brook, N J, educated at Raritan Valley Community College, received a B.A. from Salem College, W.Va., and a M.A. from The U of Notre Dame. He is a full-time Creative Writing and Drama teacher in New Jersey. For more information see CONTEMPORARY AUTHORS & WHO'S WHO IN AMERICA online in your local library.

* Also handled by SAMUEL FRENCH. Consult our Basic Catalogue of Plays our website at SAMUELFRENCH.COM and/or our most recent supplement for details.

ACT ONE

Scene:

1. Love among the Impressionists — 2 Females, 2 Males
2. Dating In The Planetarium * — 1 Female
3. The Forgery or Boating with the Spanish Singer, a Woman with a Parrot, and Manet — 3 Female, 2 Males
4. The Penitent Magdalen * — 1 Female
5. Oh, Those Antiquities! — 2 Females, 2 Males
6. The Curator * — 1 Female or Male
7. Fertility God Fugue — 3 Females, 2 Males

INTERMISSION

ACT TWO

Scene:

1. The Self Portrait * — 1 Male
2. Hanging With The Tapestries — 3 Females, 2 Males
3. The Drawing Room Guard's Big Lie * — 1 Female or Male
4. 1-555-HELP-ART — 2 Females, 1 Male
5. Misguided Tour * — 1 Female
6. Framed — 1 Male, 1 Female

The 13 one acts can be performed by 3f, 2m or by as many as 36 actors. Genders may be changed. Please see production notes for more information.

(7 Plays, 6 Monologues*)

PRODUCTION NOTES

Casting is extremely flexible. And since this play is 13 comedies, there are many ways this play may be presented. It can be performed with as few as 5 or as many as 36. Feel free to change genders for guards, Curators, fertility gods, etc. A Catholic all girl's school in Princeton, NJ, did the play with 18 females; it was a hit and sold out! Why can't Socrates be played by a woman?

A Single Set is all that is needed. Set pieces should be kept to a minimum. The first 3 productions used only stools and minimum props. Rely on the audience and their imagination to bring the rest. They will reward you for that opportunity.

Costumes can be as simple as all wearing black and using suggested props, to elaborate costumes. Though I think Socrates (male or female) has to have a toga! Who doesn't like togas?

Projections can be used if you have the technology. It is up to you. One production did not and the audience said that they did not miss anything. One production put televisions on the side of the stage. Another had 3 large projection screens center, left & right. See my website: www.LuigiJannuzzi.com for ideas. I directed the production without any projections. I liked all of them the best.

Cut the show down if you need to. THE FORGERY should be the first to go, with HANGING WITH THE TAPESTRIES next. They are group scenes that require more ensemble work, so they are usually cut first if time is a factor. With those both cut, the play runs about one hour & 15 min. Remember, MISGUIDED TOUR can be cut in 4 to 6 parts and serve as a through line. As to the order, I feel that this is the order that the show runs best. And please keep FRAMED at the end, it will be your perfect ending.

Directing this play you will find that since this is divided into separate vignettes, the entire cast doesn't have to be there all the time, which is a lot easier on the cast and director.

The tone of the play is warm, lively and fast. Please stay away from anger. There is none of that emotion written in this play. Anger is just not funny. Frustration is, but not anger. Yet amateur actors always go right for anger, which is the easiest emotion to act, and ruin comedies all the time. Please show this paragraph to any who try. After playing anger, amateurs love to add curse words. Please do not allow that either. There are none in this play for a reason. It doesn't need any. It's a comedy.

Please go to my website and email me any comments, questions or pictures. I'd love to post them on my site to brag about your production and creativity. So if you are using a scene for forensics, a one act competition or in a collection of one acts, I'd love to hear how it went.

The Art work is listed on my website: www.LuigiJannuzzi.com

All photos enclosed in this script were taken by me.

Raising the awareness of Art through the use of Comedy and trying to create in a verbal medium (Theatre) a hunger for a visual medium (Paintings) is one the objects of the show.

Have fun. It was fun writing this play and directing it. Audiences howl and applaud often. From Princeton professors to a school group of 3rd graders it makes them laugh.

Break a frame!

Luigi Jannuzzi

SPECIAL THANKS TO: All at Samuel French Inc., Alleen Hussung, and the late William (Bill) Talbot, Michael Gallagher for the cover art, Ralph Sevush & David Faux @ The Dramatist Guild, The Author's Guild, Nancy E. Wolff, Esq., @ Cowan, DeBaets, Abrahams & Sheppard LLP, Luis Angulo of La_Designs, Branan Whitehead, Joe Devito III, Weist-Barron Studios, 35 w 45 Street & Manager Charles F. Wagner IV, Lauren Embrey & Lindsay Harwell for all of their rehearsal support, Emma RosenBlum: New York Magazine for giving us a #1 pick in "Midsummer in Midtown," LucyAnn Dunlap: US 1 News, Clare Trapasso: NY Daily News, Dr. Roberta E. Zlokower: RobertaontheArts.com, Susan Van Dongen: Time Off @ The Princeton Packet, Stephanie Murg: Chelsea Now News, NYC, Deborah S. Greenhut at OOBR.com, Jo Ann Rosen at NYTheatre.com, Pete Ernst & The Waterfront Ensemble/NJ Dramatists for supporting new works. Leecia Manning who directed the first reading @ The DeBaun, Hoboken, NJ. Karen Greatti, Terri Campion, Jeff Baskin, Jeff Biehl, Lisa Rudin, Marcia Finn, Cynthia Granville, Michael Giorgio, Alice Connorton, Tim Barrett, Jennifer Kotrba, Judy Bard, David Tyson, David Walters, Joan Saporta, Michael Cleeff, Michael & Candice Gallagher, Marilyn Anker, Robert Rund, and the cast and crew of the PEDDIE PLAYER'S award-winning production of this play.

Jewel Seehaus-Fisher & NJTEC for a reading @ Playwright's Theatre of NJ Janice Baldwin & The Stuart Country Day School of the Sacred Heart, Princeton NJ. their Cast and Crew for the first high school production. Gabor & Susanne Barabas for presenting the play @ NJREP in Long Branch, NJ. Charles F. Wagner IV who directed a reading @ Villagers Theatre, Franklin, NJ

NJTheater.com & Chris Fitzgerald for the Perry Award for the Production of Best Original Play in NJ.

Elizabeth Rothan for directing the Midtown International Festival production. Mario Fratti for all his advice & confidence, The New Jersey State Council On The Arts, The National Endowment for the Humanities, The Geraldine R. Dodge Foundation, Helen Waren Mayer, John Chatterton, Emileena Pedigo, Bob Ost, Glory Sims Bowen, Judd Hollander & the Midtown International Theatre Festival Staff,

And The Metropolitan Museum Of Art.

"The mind can not absorb what the rear end can not endure."
                                                    - Moliere

LOVE AMONG THE IMPRESSIONISTS

CAST

(In Order Of Appearance)

RAPHAEL

RACHEL (In picture)

MONA

MICHAEL (In picture)

LOVE AMONG THE IMPRESSIONISTS was first produced by The Peddie Players at The Peddie School in Hightstown, NJ in July 2005. The play was directed by Michael Gallagher; produced by Robert Rund; set design by John Lucs; lighting design by Marilyn Anker; Crew and Advisors: Lynn Schreffler, Robert Gargiullo & Roby McClellan. The cast was as follows:

RAPHAEL.....................................Bruce Clough

RACHEL (In picture) ....Catherine Rowe

MONA..Bonnie Powell

MICHAEL (In picture) ....Tom Stevenson

It was presented by the Metropolitan Theatre Company at New Jersey Repertory Company, Long Branch, NJ in July 2005. The play was directed by Luigi Jannuzzi; Executive producer Gabor Barabas; Artistic Director Suzanne Barabas. The cast was as follows:

RAPHAEL.....................................Ben Masur

RACHEL (In picture) ....Robin Marie Thomas

MONA..Liz Zazzi

MICHAEL (In picture) ....Joseph Franchini

It was produced by The Metropolitan Theatre Company in New York City as a selection of The Midtown International Theatre Festival, at the Workshop Theatre Main Stage, 312 West 36th St, 4th Floor, on July 2007. Executive Producer John Chatterton; Managing Director Emileena Pedigo; Artistic Director Glory Sims Bowen; Marketing Director Bob Ost. The play was directed by Elizabeth Rothan; Assistant directed by Lauren Embrey; produced by Luigi Jannuzzi/Elizabeth Rothan; lighting design by

Alan Kanevsky; projection by Eric Christopher Hoelle. The cast was as follows:

RAPHAEL....................................Billy Lane

RACHEL (In picture) ....Kristin Carter

MONA...Emily Beatty *

MICHAEL (In picture) ....Joseph Franchini

*Also appearing as Mona: Lauren Embrey

(*Music begins and lights rise on two paintings in a museum. One is of a young woman, the other painting is of a young man. Entering the door of the room and stopping there is* **RAPHAEL** *with a single rose.*)

RAPHAEL. Oh. (*Pause.*) There you are. How I've missed you. How I've thought only of you all night.

(**WOMAN**'s *face in painting puckers* **HER** *lips three times, resumes pose.*)

RAPHAEL. Oh. (*Pause.*) Don't tease me. Don't do that to me.

(**WOMAN** *puckers* **HER** *lips three more times, resumes pose.*)

RAPHAEL. Oh. (*Pause.*) My heart. The sword in my heart says, "Please remove."

RACHEL. (*Only moving mouth.*) Why do you make me wait so?

RAPHAEL. You know how important you are to me.

RACHEL. I suffer.

RAPHAEL. Don't say that.

RACHEL. All night.

RAPHAEL. I suffer more.

RACHEL. No. You are with you, I am not.

RAPHAEL. I brought you a flower.

RACHEL. I can not smell.

RAPHAEL. You can look.

15

RACHEL. I don't want to.

RAPHAEL. (*Throws flower away.*) It is ugly compared to you.

RACHEL. Tell me more.

RAPHAEL. This museum is unworthy of you.

RACHEL. More.

RAPHAEL. Mona Lisa is a sketch.

RACHEL. More.

RAPHAEL. I want to bring you home and paint you again.

RACHEL. Oh. I like this.

RAPHAEL. I want to put the colors all over you.

RACHEL. What color?

RAPHAEL. Red.

RACHEL. OOoh.

RAPHAEL. I want to smear the reds.

RACHEL. Where?

RAPHAEL. Wherever.

RACHEL. Oh, you make me run.

(**MONA,** *a young woman enters and crosses to painting of young man.*)

RAPHAEL. I want to stretch your canvas.

RACHEL. Mmmmm.

RAPHAEL. I want to laminate you.

MONA. Hi Michael, it's me.

RACHEL. (*To* **RAPHAEL.**) Psst.

MICHAEL. Go away.

RAPHAEL. I want to uh,...

RACHEL. Psst.

MONA. You don't mean that.

RAPHAEL. What?

MONA. Michael, listen to me.

RACHEL. (*Motioning to other party.*) Listen.

MONA. You are all I think about.

MICHAEL. Get a life.

MONA. You are my life, my perfect image of what could be.

MICHAEL. I don't exist.

MONA. You do.

MICHAEL. I'm a remnant of a love affair.

MONA. No.

MICHAEL. Let it rest.

MONA. Never.

MICHAEL. Then at least leave me alone.

MONA. I just want to say hello.

MICHAEL. That's not true. You sold me, now let me hang here in peace.

MONA. You're angry about that.

MICHAEL. It's the best thing that ever happened. You think I liked hanging over your bed? Cut me a break.

MONA. I told you I needed the money.

MICHAEL. I love it here. You're just using this as an excuse to talk to me.

MONA. You forgive me?

MICHAEL. I forgive you, get lost.

MONA. No you don't.

MICHAEL. I am now going to ignore you.

RACHEL. She comes here every day.

RAPHAEL. No.

RACHEL. Twice on weekends.

RAPHAEL. Sad.

MONA. You can't ignore me for long.

RAPHAEL. She's lonely.

MICHAEL. Watch me.

RAPHAEL. She's attractive.

RACHEL. Don't get any ideas.

RAPHAEL. Well, I know her. You know that don't you?

MONA. I created you.

MICHAEL. I don't love you.

RACHEL. I forbid you to talk to her.

RAPHAEL. She's a very nice person.

MONA. After this exhibit closes, you may need me.

RACHEL. She's obsessed.

RAPHAEL. I like that in a woman.

MICHAEL. Listen to me. You sold me. I don't belong to you. Now get out of the way so others can admire me.

MONA. That hurts me. I mean, that really hurts me.

MICHAEL. I am now officially ignoring you.

RAPHAEL. Mona?

> (**YOUNG WOMAN** *turns.*)

MONA. Raphael, you were right.

RAPHAEL Right about what?

> (**MONA** *slips into* **RAPHAEL'S** *arms.*)

MONA. I don't know why I created him.

RACHEL. Hey.

RAPHAEL. It's okay.

RACHEL. Hey, watch it there.

MONA. They want everything, you give them everything, then when they're successful they won't even look down on you.

RAPHAEL. Perhaps that's what you intended.

MONA. You know, you're right.

(**MONA** *to painting of* **YOUNG MAN.**)

The real you is a jerk, what made me think the image would be any better.

MICHAEL. Bounces off me, returns to you.

MONA. I should just go get a can of blue and wipe you out.

MICHAEL. I am not going to give you the satisfaction of yelling, "Guard."

RAPHAEL. Mona, let him go.

MICHAEL. How can she? A peace warrant says she can't harass her ex anymore. God knows she tried. A two time offender standing there before us. Right Mona? So she paints me and obsesses. I can't get off the wall to get a warrant, so I'm stuck with her. I thank God everyday that she wrecked her car and had to sell me for the money to buy another one.

RAPHAEL. This is a picture of your ex-husband?

MONA. He's almost bald now.

MICHAEL. He went bald worrying about her stalking him.

MONA. Oh shut up.

MICHAEL. Call Park city, Utah police. They've got candids.

MONA. This was about 15 years ago.

RAPHAEL. In your picture he's very handsome.

MICHAEL. Please don't feed the fire.

MONA. (*To* **RAPHAEL.**) He even talks like him, do you know that?

RAPHAEL. They all do.

MONA. It's so frightening, isn't it?

RAPHAEL. Mona, let's go get some lunch.

RACHEL. No.

RAPHAEL. Rachel, we're only going to have lunch.

RACHEL. I said, "No."

MONA. I wish my paintings would act like that.

MICHAEL. Please, take her to lunch.

RAPHAEL. Mine's of a former mistress.

MONA. Really?

RAPHAEL. Had to break off quickly. She called my wife.

MONA. I didn't know you were married?

RAPHAEL. I was for a year. Then I started doing sculpture. My hands went one way, my wife went the other.

MONA. It's hard to do sculpture and have another relationship.

RAPHAEL. Too much touching.

MONA. Definitely.

RAPHAEL Want to go to the usual haunt?

MONA. I love it there.

RAPHAEL. Rachel, I'll be back.

RACHEL. I can't believe you're doing this to me. Right in front of me.

RAPHAEL. Rachel, I'm just going to have lunch.

RACHEL. That's how we started.

RAPHAEL. It's not the same.

RACHEL. A thought.

RAPHAEL. Rachel.

RACHEL. A little sketch on a napkin.

RAPHAEL. Listen to me.

RACHEL. Then all the promises.

RAPHAEL. I'm talking a turkey sandwich.

RACHEL. You won't come back today, I know it.

RAPHAEL. I'll be back in three hours.

MICHAEL. I'll keep her company.

RAPHAEL. Talk to him.

RACHEL. I should talk to him.

RAPHAEL. Please.

RACHEL. You don't care?

RAPHAEL. We'll be back.

(**RAPHAEL** *and* **MONA** *exit.*)

RACHEL. He doesn't care.

MICHAEL. Ah…they're all like that.

RACHEL. I know he likes her.

MICHAEL. They create us for their needs; they don't care what we need.

RACHEL. I need him.

MICHAEL. You need a man.

RACHEL. We talk so much.

MICHAEL. You need a one dimensional man like me.

RACHEL. She's going to take my place.

MICHAEL. You need a man who values words. A man like him wants touching.

RACHEL. What am I going to do?

MICHAEL. Well, if you were smart, you'd look to your left.

RACHEL. I don't know what you mean.

MICHAEL. I mean, ever since I've been hanging here, I've been looking at you.

RACHEL. Stop it.

MICHAEL. I have.

RACHEL. You have?

MICHAEL. Who hasn't? Everyone who comes into the room gravitates to you.

RACHEL. That's not true.

MICHAEL. Oh, I think you know it is true.

RACHEL. No.

MICHAEL. I can't keep my eyes off you either.

RACHEL. You make my frame shake.

MICHAEL. Oooh. Say that again.

RACHEL. What?

MICHAEL. Say that again, "You make my frame shake."

RACHEL. Why?

MICHAEL. Say it again.

RACHEL. You make my frame shake.

MICHAEL. Oooh. I love how you say that.

RACHEL. Really?

MICHAEL. Yes.

RACHEL. OOooh. I think I like you too.

MICHAEL. OOooh. Really?

(*Lights begin to fade.*)

RACHEL. Yes. Now are you a watercolor or a pastel?

MICHAEL. I'm an,…oil.

RACHEL. Me too!

BOTH TOGETHER

OOhhhhhh.

(*Blackout.*)

PROPS

Raphael needs a single flower, perhaps a rose.

Exhibits at the Metropolitan Museum of Art in New York
that corresponds to the scene:
LOVE AMONG THE IMPRESSIONISTS

Pierre-Auguste Renoir
"By The Seashore," 1883

Pierre-Auguste Renoir
"Hyacinthe-Eugene Meunier," 1877

See website: *www.LuigiJannuzzi.com*
for pictures and links.

Pierre-Auguste Renoir
" A waitress at Duval's Restaurant," 1875

Edgar Degas
"James-Jacques-Joseph Tissot," 1868

DATING IN THE PLANETARIUM

CAST

JOSEPHINE

DATING IN THE PLANETARIUM was first produced by The
Peddie Players at The Peddie School in Hightstown, NJ in
July 2005. The play was directed by Michael Gallagher;
produced by Robert Rund; set design by John Lucs; lighting design by Marilyn Anker; Crew and Advisors: Lynn
Schreffler, Robert Gargiullo & Roby McClellan. The cast
was as follows:

JOSEPHINE..................................Candace Gallagher

It was presented by the Metropolitan Theatre Company at
New Jersey Repertory Company, Long Branch, NJ in July
2005. The play was directed by Luigi Jannuzzi; Executive
producer Gabor Barabas; Artistic Director Suzanne Barabas. The cast was as follows:

JOSEPHINE..................................Stephanie Dorian

It was produced by The Metropolitan Theatre Company
in New York City as a selection of The Midtown Interna-
tional Theatre Festival, at the Workshop Theatre Main
Stage, 312 West 36th St, 4th Floor, on July 2007. Executive
Producer John Chatterton; Managing Director Emileena
Pedigo; Artistic Director Glory Sims Bowen; Marketing
Director Bob Ost. The play was directed by Elizabeth
Rothan; Assistant directed by Lauren Embrey; produced
by Luigi Jannuzzi/Elizabeth Rothan; lighting design by
Alan Kanevsky; projection by Eric Christopher Hoelle. The
cast was as follows:

JOSEPHINE..................................Dawn E. McGee

(*Lights rise on* **WOMAN**.)

As soon as I got the job at the museum, everyone told me, "Don't date anyone at work." Good advice. They usually say, "Don't dip into the company ink." Emily, in charge of Strollers in coat check says, "Don't sample the company palette."

So the first guy I date, he's a waiter in the cafeteria and part time student in Islamic art. It's a nightmare. He virtually stalked me. Gives me an armlet, it's a wrist band, knock off of an early medieval bracelet from Greater Iran, early 11th century, had four hemispheres flanking the clasp, it was gold, gorgeous. I swear it had a homing device. Besides the fact all his friends drove cabs, he could track me down in a half hour. It wasn't till I started dating Hans in Armor and Weapons that he accepted the armlet back and left me alone. Then we found out the armlet was early 11th century, he said he "borrowed it." I think his arraignment's next week.

Then Hans, big, blonde, built like the Alps, an expert in Swiss daggers. That should have been a big clue. Hans' favorite dagger is the one that has, on the ornamental scabbard, the very appropriately chosen theme, "The Dance of Death." Another glaring clue!

First date Hans said we'd go out the first day of Doe season. I figured we'd walk around the forest with binoculars, look at female deer who must come out that day to do,... God knows what. So I prepare a picnic basket, wine,... Hans shows up in camouflage. Hans

29

has two medieval crossbows, including his mom's favorite made of strips of horn and whalebone which she graciously allowed me to use. I start crying. Drop the basket. Mumbled something about Bambi's mom. In the parking lot, Han's van is filled with his friends, both male and females, they're drinking beer, yelling things like, "Come on Hans, they'll all be dead before we get there." I swear I think one of the women had one of those hats on her head with the horns, it was very frightening.

Then I met Henry Limone', Medieval Art. Quiet, religious, did his doctorate on South Netherlands 15th Century cribs of the infant Jesus. These are one foot by one foot devotional objects given to nuns taking vows. Inside the bed there's usually a relic. He seemed the sweetest, most sensitive guy. My parents loved him. We dated three months. I'm just going to tell you one thing. He kept insisting that I get really short hair. I didn't mind. Then he wanted me to dress up like a choir boy. Enough said. Then I found his magazines, met his lover Albert. He started crying. It was sad. He still bakes me cookies sometimes, we have lunch first Wednesday of every month. Which catapulted me into my wild period with Alberto from Abstract. Drugs were involved, a lot of things I'd rather not mention. A lot of clubbing. For nine months it was an intense, surrealistic, fabric of faces and torsos, totemic figures in strobing soft blue. There were maybe 30- 35 Lear Jet rides to explore the positive/negative relationships of our allegorical decent. We hung around with the Pre Roman Art of Italy people a lot. Talk about decadence. They make Caligula's parties look like a bar- mitzvah.

Then I had the nervous breakdown. I lost it. I was conducting a tour for sixth graders in American Paintings. I was describing that painting "THE APPROACHING THUNDER STORM" by Martin Johnson Heade. You know that? (*Pause.*) I thought I saw lightening bolts in the picture. I told the kids to duck. They did. Then I thought the man in the painting turned around and said, "Run for your life!" I screamed, "Run for your lives!" All the kids ran. I ran. I hid behind the giant Emanuel Gottlieb Leutze painting of "WASHINGTON CROSSING THE DELAWARE."

They called the police. I wouldn't come out. A crowd formed. The stalker-waiter guy was the first person there, I started screaming. Hans appeared, tried to pry my hands loose, I started kicking. Alberto tried to get me to drink a mild sedative, I knocked the drink out of his hand. Henry, remember Henry from Medieval Art, he actually came behind the canvas and calmed me down a little till Emily, you remember Emily? She's in charge of strollers at the coat check? Well, Emily convinced me to sit in a wheel chair and she'd roll me away to safety. I agreed. (*Pause.*) I'm out on disability. I'm now dating a guy in the American Wing. Todd. Very conservative. He thinks Victorian, Rococo revival love seats are radical. He's about as much fun as a colonial clock. But yesterday I met Zeke, he's cute, an astronomer at one of the nearby planetariums. He's way out there. Wears a cape, has a cane with Galileo's face on the staff. Pretty neat huh?

I don't know, maybe Emily's right, I shouldn't "Sample the company's palette," maybe I should expand myself to the universe. Though I can't afford another breakdown. I'll have to think about this!

(*Lights fade, Blackout.*)

Exhibits at the Metropolitan Museum of Art in New York
that corresponds to the scene:
DATING IN THE PLANETARIUM

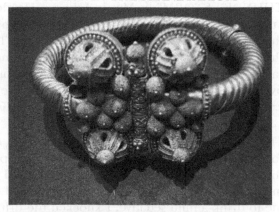

Iranian "Armlet"
Gurgan, Iran, 1030 A.D.

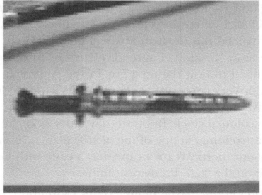

"Dagger" (Schweizerdolch), 1567

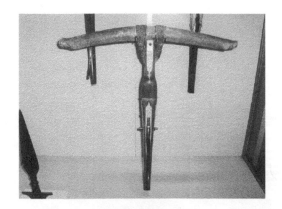

"Hunting Crossbow"
German, 1460

"Crib of the Infant Jesus"
South Netherlandish, 15 C.

Jackson Pollock
"Pasiphae" 1943 or "Autumn Rhythm, " 1950

Martin Johnson Heade, 1859
"The Coming Storm" renamed "The Approaching Thunder Storm"

Emanuel Gottlieb Leutze
"Washington Crossing the Delaware" 1851

"Tete-a-tete"
Victorian Rococo Revival Love Seat, 1863

(All are mentioned in scene.)
See website: *www.LuigiJannuzzi.com*
for pictures and links.

THE FORGERY
or
BOATING WITH THE SPANISH SINGER, A WOMAN WITH A PARROT, AND MANET

CAST

(In Order Of Appearance)

SPANISH SINGER.

LADY (VICKY) WITH PARROT

PARROT VOICE (Done by Lady w/Parrot)

MAN IN BOAT

WOMAN IN BOAT

GUARD

CURATOR (May be intercom)

THE FORGERY or *BOATING WITH THE SPANISH SINGER, A WOMAN WITH A PARROT, AND MANET* was first presented by the Metropolitan Theatre Company at New Jersey Repertory Company, Long Branch, NJ in July 2005. The play was directed by Luigi Jannuzzi; Executive producer Gabor Barabas; Artistic Director Suzanne Barabas. The cast was as follows:

SPANISH SINGER........................Joseph Franchini

LADY (VICKY) WITH PARROT .....Stephanie Dorian

PARROT VOICE (Done by Lady) ... Stephanie Dorian

MAN IN BOAT...............................Marc Geller

WOMAN IN BOAT ....Robin Marie Thomas

GUARD ....Ben Masur

CURATOR (May be intercom) ...Liz Zazzi

(*Lights rise on* **SPANISH SINGER** *playing cards with a* **FRENCH MAN** *in a bamboo hat. A* **FRENCH WOMAN** *leans over the* **FRENCH MAN'S** *shoulder. Another* **WOMAN IN LONG GOWN** (**VICKY**) *is dusting a large frame. Against the wall three large blank frames are hanging.*)

(**SPANISH SINGER** *puts cards on table, picks up guitar and strums while talk singing.*)

SINGER. "I'll bet ya,...I'll beat ya,...in life and in cards."

MAN IN BOAT. I'm callin' you.

SINGER. "I bet ya,...I'm not the for....gery."

MAN IN BOAT. Yea, well, it ain't us.

VICKY. Well I'm surely not the forgery.

PARROT. Not the forgery.

(**SPANISH SINGER** *puts down guitar, picks up cards.*)

SINGER. Steve, says it's one of us.

VICKY. What does Steven know, he's just a guard.

PARROT. Just a guard.

WOMAN IN BOAT. Manet became a true impressionist when he created me.

MAN IN BOAT. No, don't do that.

WOMAN IN BOAT. I'm just saying, we have light colors, a raised viewpoint.

MAN IN BOAT. We have no need to defend ourselves.

WOMAN IN BOAT. I'm just saying.

39

MAN IN BOAT. We are well documented, we know what we
  are.

SINGER. But it doesn't matter that we know we're not forg-
  eries, what matters is what they think, and what they
  think they know.

VICKY. That's the truth.

PARROT. That's the truth.

VICKY. (*To* **PARROT**.) That's enough.

SINGER. Am I right?

MAN IN BOAT. Don't get her started.

VICKY. When Manet first exhibited me, critics said I was a
  bad painting.

MAN IN BOAT. We've only heard this how many times?

VICKY. Till everyone

ALL. At the Salon, in Eighteen Hundred and sixty six,
  thought that I was a bad picture, including Edouard
  Manet.

VICKY. Don't taunt me.

WOMAN IN BOAT. We're not taunting you.

MAN IN BOAT. We're just bored.

  (*All laugh but* **VICKY**.)

VICKY. Yes well, we'll see who's bored when we find out
  who's the forgery and has the canvas ripped from their
  frame.

  (*Silence.*)

WOMAN IN BOAT. That wasn't a very nice thing to say at a
  time like this.

  (**FRENCH MAN** *puts down cards.*)

MAN IN BOAT. Three Jacks. (or "Trois Jacks.")

VICKY. Truth has its moment, my dear.

SINGER. Three Queens. (or "Tres Queens.")

VICKY. And while we're still lounging in shock mode.

PARROT. Shock mode.

VICKY. Quiet. Did everyone partake in the curator's casual newsletter?

SINGER. I heard something.

VICKY. The one the patrons were reading this afternoon that announced that one of us, I was straining, could not catch which, was chosen to travel to Paris for a summer grand gala on our beloved master at either the Muse'e d'Orsay or the Louvre.

WOMAN IN BOAT. Oh, wouldn't that be wonderful.

SINGER. Hey you better watch it, they may hang you in the same room with that scandalous picture of that naked woman with a parrot by who was it?

VICKY. Courbet.

SINGER. Yea, Courbet.

VICKY. I'm quite comfortable with my sexuality, thank you.

MAN IN BOAT. Pardon me.

VICKY. And I have much more than that woman.

MAN IN BOAT. No.

WOMAN IN BOAT. No.

SINGER. Not true.

VICKY. I am Manet's allegory to the five senses.

(**ALL** *rise.*)

SINGER. Well don't we believe everything we read in the guidebook.

MAN IN BOAT. I have to get some sleep.

VICKY. I am smell.

ALL. Violets.

VICKY. Touch and Sight

ALL. Monocle.

VICKY. Hearing

ALL. Parrot.

VICKY. and taste

ALL. Orange.

SINGER. And you could be a forgery.

(**THEY** *all laugh.*)

VICKY. Laugh all you want, I'll send greeting from Paris.

SINGER. Hey now, how come I can't be an allegory.

WOMAN IN BOAT. I think you'd make a wonderful allegory.

SINGER. I have smell.

MAN IN BOAT. He doesn't bathe.

SINGER. I was thinking the two onions in the picture.

WOMAN IN BOAT. Your squashed cigarette.

SINGER. Even better.

MAN IN BOAT. You have hearing.

SINGER. A guitar is hearing.

WOMAN IN BOAT. Music.

SINGER. Exactly.

MAN IN BOAT. Taste.

SINGER. I have a red jug of wine. It tastes good.

VICKY. What about sight?

SINGER. I'm a flashy guy.

WOMAN IN BOAT. You're singing a song, you're a sight.

SINGER. I even have a red strap,...that's noted in the guide book.

MAN IN BOAT. That's a sight.

SINGER. Sure.

VICKY. What about touch?

SINGER. What about it?

VICKY. What do you have for touch?

SINGER. I'm touching my guitar. My touch even creates,... music.

VICKY. You used music for hearing.

SINGER. Then uh,...

VICKY. You don't have anything for touch.

SINGER. Sure I do.

VICKY. What?

SINGER. Well that's where my rumpled pants come in.

VICKY. You're rude and demented.

MAN IN BOAT. And maybe a forgery.

SINGER. Gee that would pretty much round me out, wouldn't it?

(*All but woman with parrot laughs.*)

And I have speed, since Manet painted me in just 2 hours! So I have even another dimension.

VICKY. Someone's coming.

(**THEY** *all jump into frames, assume pose.*)

(**GUARD** *enters with a folded white sheet and a black sheet.*)

MAN IN BOAT. Steve.

VICKY. Steven.

SINGER. Stevie, what'd you hear?

(**THEY** *begin climbing out of the frames.*)

GUARD. Stay in your frames, the curator's going to be here in a moment.

(**ALL** *are out and up to* **STEVE**.)

MAN IN BOAT. This time of night?

GUARD. It's important.

SINGER. It can't wait till morning?

GUARD. They're making the move before the museum opens.

(**ALL** *gasp.*)

VICKY. What move?

GUARD. Two moves.

(**ALL** *gasp.*)

WOMAN IN BOAT. Oh my God. Is it us, Steve?

SINGER. Who's the forgery?

GUARD. I don't know.

MAN IN BOAT. You know.

GUARD. I honestly don't know.

WOMAN IN BOAT. You have a hint?

GUARD. Honest to God, I do not know. As I told everyone I saw on the paper the words, "The forged Manet." That's all I saw.

SINGER. And it's in this room?

GUARD. In this room.

SINGER. So it's one of us.

GUARD. One of you.

WOMAN IN BOAT. You're positive?

GUARD. God as my judge. This room, only the three of you, it's gotta be one of you.

VICKY. And the one that's going to Paris for the summer?

GUARD. Again, all I know it's one of you. It was in the curator's newsletter. But he's on his way he wants both paintings moved before we open.

VICKY. I can't take the tension.

GUARD. He gave me two sheets.

MAN IN BOAT. What sheets?

WOMAN IN BOAT. What are you talking about?

GUARD. This white one goes over the one to Paris.

SINGER. And the black?

GUARD. The other.

VICKY. It's a shroud.

SINGER. The black goes over the forgery?

GUARD. He's taking the stairs up, I took the elevator, he's going to tell me which. Now please get back in your frames. This is beyond my control, I have nothing to do with this. You know I would do anything for any of you, there's nothing I can do.

(*Over to door.*)

Here he comes.

(**CURATOR** *enters, or intercom comes on.*)

CURATOR. Steven, you have the sheets?

GUARD. Yes Sir.

CURATOR. Alright. let me see. The white sheet, which is the painting that will accompany me to Paris, please put over Ms. Victorine Meurent.

GUARD. The woman with the parrot, Sir?

CURATOR. Yes, Victorine, will be meeting her other three selves. She posed for Manet's Olympia, have you ever seen that, Steven?

GUARD. No.

CURATOR. In the Museé d'orsay.

GUARD. I hope to someday, Sir.

CURATOR. She's naked as a babe.

GUARD. I'd like to see that, Sir.

CURATOR. And also for "Le Dejeuner sur l'herbe." So this summer at the Museé d'orsay, sort of a triptych of Vic.

(**CURATOR** *laughs,* **STEVE** *tries.*)

(**CURATOR'S** *phone rings.*)

Excuse me, I'll be right back.

(**CURATOR** *clicks off intercom or exits talking into phone.*)

VICKY. I'm going to Parie!

SINGER. It can't be.

WOMAN IN BOAT. It's not right.

VICKY. Yes, we're going back!

PARROT. Going back!

SINGER. I was his first debut at the Salon.

MAN IN BOAT. It's wrong.

WOMAN IN BOAT. What can we do?

MAN IN BOAT. There's nothing we can do.

VICKY. To Parie!

PARROT. Parie! Parie!

MAN IN BOAT. Hey, shut the parrot up, Vicky.

VICKY. Oh, and since when are we bastions of etiquette?

SINGER. Vicky, just cool it for a few minutes, okay?

GUARD. He's coming back.

CURATOR. (*Into phone.*) Bye bye.

> (**CURATOR** *comes back on intercom or enters room while folding phone.*)

Okay, Steven, where were we?

GUARD. At the forgery, Sir.

CURATOR. What are you talking about?

GUARD. I'm sorry. I saw it on your notepad, and then when you told me to get the two sheets I felt that confirmed it.

CURATOR. Steven, where on my notepad does it say "forgery"?

GUARD. It says, "The forged Manet."

CURATOR. My notepad says, "The forced Manet"

GUARD. Oh. It's not a "g", Sir? "F", "O", "R", "G".

CURATOR. "F", "O", "R", "*C*". Forced. The SPANISH SINGER is going to Paris, for an exhibit on what I call "forced work," work deliberately created in one sitting. Did you know, Steven, this painting was created in two hours by Manet.

GUARD. I heard.

CURATOR. Speed. That's what separates this painting from the rest.

GUARD. Oh really, Sir.

CURATOR. His fingers moving, his leg up. That's what separates a lot of the "forced" works, He's vibrant.

GUARD. Oh he is.

CURATOR. Put the black sheet on our Spanish friend.

GUARD. Yes Sir.

CURATOR. See you tomorrow.

GUARD. See you tomorrow, Sir.

> (**CURATOR** *clicks off intercom or exits.* **STEVEN** *unfolds one of the sheets. Pause. All* **CHARACTERS** *lean forward staring at* **GUARD**)

> Now, I know what you're all thinking. What a dope I am. And you're right. And I'm sorry. I'm very sorry.

> (**FRENCH MAN** *jumps out of frame, heads toward light switch on wall.*)

SINGER. Get the light.

GUARD. I said I'm sorry.

VICKY. I thank you, Steven.

PARROT. Thank you, Steven

> (**SPANISH MAN** *out of frame.*)

MAN IN BOAT. I'll cover this side.

VICKY. I am so grateful.

PARROT. So grateful.

VICKY. To go to Paris.

PARROT. Go to Paris.

WOMAN IN BOAT. You put us through hell, Steve.

GUARD. Wait a minute. Listen.

(*Lights go out.*)

SINGER. Get him.

GUARD. Let me go.

MAN IN BOAT. I got him.

VICKY. I'm going to Paris!

GUARD. Get off me.

MAN IN BOAT. How could you?

PARROT. Going to Paris.

SINGER. Get him.

WOMAN IN BOAT. Let me hit him too.

GUARD. Stop it. Stop it.

PARROT. Goin' to Paris!

GUARD. OW!

MAN IN BOAT. Take that.

SINGER. That.

GUARD. OW!

WOMAN IN BOAT. And that.

GUARD. Get off me!

PARROT. Goin' to Paris!

GUARD. Get back in your frames! Guaaaaaard!

(*End of play.*)

PROPS AND COSTUMES

SPANISH SINGER.....guitar and black hat.

WOMAN W/PARROT.....duster & Parrot on stand

FRENCH MAN.........Straw hat, deck of cards

GUARDS wear blue blazer, blue pants, white shirt, maroon tie, black shoes.

SET

Stools can be used in the background instead of frames.

Exhibits at the Metropolitan Museum of Art in New York
that corresponds to the scene:

THE FORGERY

or

BOATING WITH THE SPANISH SINGER,
A WOMAN WITH A PARROT, AND MANET

Edouard Manet
"The Spanish Singer" 1860

Edouard Manet
"Young Lady in 1866" 1866

Edouard Manet
"Boating" 1874

(Above paintings are in the scene.)
(Below paintings are mentioned.)
Gustave Courbet
"Woman with a Parrot"

Edouard Manet
"Olympia" *

Edouard Manet
"Le Dejeuner sur l'herbe" or "Luncheon on the Grass" *

* Both at *The Musée d'Orsay, Paris, France*

See website: *www.LuigiJannuzzi.com*
for pictures and links.

THE PENITENT MAGDALEN

CAST

MAGDALEN

THE PENITENT MAGDALEN was first produced by The Peddie Players at The Peddie School in Hightstown, NJ in July 2005. The play was directed by Michael Gallagher; produced by Robert Rund; set design by John Lucs; lighting design by Marilyn Anker; Crew and Advisors: Lynn Schreffler, Robert Gargiullo & Roby McClellan. The cast was as follows:

MAGDALEN ....Catherine Rowe

It was presented by the Metropolitan Theatre Company at New Jersey Repertory Company, Long Branch, NJ in July 2005. The play was directed by Luigi Jannuzzi; Executive producer Gabor Barabas; Artistic Director Suzanne Barabas. The cast was as follows:

MAGDALEN ....Liz Zazzi

It was produced by The Metropolitan Theatre Company in New York City as a selection of The Midtown International Theatre Festival, at the Workshop Theatre Main Stage, 312 West 36th St, 4th Floor, on July 2007. Executive Producer John Chatterton; Managing Director Emileena Pedigo; Artistic Director Glory Sims Bowen; Marketing Director Bob Ost. The play was directed by Elizabeth Rothan; Assistant directed by Lauren Embrey; produced by Luigi Jannuzzi/Elizabeth Rothan; lighting design by Alan Kanevsky; projection by Eric Christopher Hoelle. The cast was as follows:

MAGDALEN ....Kristin Carter

(**WOMAN** *enters very frustrated. Please don't play this angry. Frustrated is funny, angry is not.*)

I'm going to talk to the curator of this museum. I'm going right now. I am so frustrated. I am getting the Curator of this museum to change the title of the painting I'm in. Because I'm sorry. I am very very sorry. And my question is:

(*Frustrated, not angry.*)

For how many hundreds of years do I have to apologize?

(*just a little lower.*)

I never hurt anyone, but myself, being a prostitute. Yet why am I the focal point of repentance for this entire civilization? Why am I the archetypal sinner, the "whipping girl" of "Don't let your daughter be this?"

(*Normal tone.*)

And I feel, it is because of the title of my portrait. The title is: "The Penitent Magdalen." Penitent: "Feeling remorse for sins committed."

(*Pause.*)

Now that brands me. My only solace is that my painter, Georges De La Tour, chose that you only see the side of my face. I'm very glad you don't see my entire face. Even in the mirror I stare into, you can not see my entire face. Thank you Georges. Quite frankly, I am ashamed of what I did and what I was. But is that what the painting is about? In the painting, I am at the moment of my epiphany of what a terrible life "we" are leading.

I say "we" because I have 3 sisters. Georges painted four of us Maddalen's. That was nice of him. So there's company in the demand. And we all feel the same way. We feel, I feel: why at that point of conversion can't we, I be called Saint Magdalen, or just Mary Magdalen? Why accent the moment before the point of change, when the point of change, is what this painting is about? Or is this really a woman's issue? Is that what this is? Is it: "Once a prostitute, always a prostitute?" You're branded and that sticks. No matter what else occurs in one's life. No matter if later in life, like I do, you do become "a Saint." Oh no,...you still have to wear the prostitute name tag over the Saint one?

(*SHE walks half way across the stage, stops, and to a man in the front row.*)

Or maybe it's just men's fascination with prostitutes, maybe that's what it is. Which is funny because there are a lot of prostitutes in this museum. On the canvases, I mean.

(*Pause.*)

Prostitutes have been models from time immemorial. In fact, you should see the number of prostitutes on these walls. You would be amazed when you look at the breakdown of women painted and what they are,... Wives, a few, mothers,...a couple,....but prostitutes, (*Pause.*) a lot. Sometimes I wonder whether it's a God thing with artists to try and take something of little societal value and suddenly thus change worth through brush stokes. Setting themselves up more godly than God. Or at least the doer of God's ultimate will.

(*Pause.*)

I've been thinking about all sorts of things like this since that moment of realization, at the mirror, that Georges painted me at. Anyway, so much about epiphanies and painted ladies.* I have an appointment with the Curator in seven minutes. Wish me luck!

(**SHE** *exits.*)

* "Painted Ladies" is a slang term for Prostitute.

Exhibits at the Metropolitan Museum of Art in New York
that corresponds to the scene:

THE PENITENT MAGDALEN

Georges De La Tour
"The Penitent Magdalen" 1643

See also:
Georges De La Tour
"Magdalen with The Smoking Flame," 1640
Los Angeles County Museum of Art

and

Georges De La Tour
"Magdalen of Night Light," 1635
Museé du Lourve, Paris

and

Georges De La Tour
"The Repentant Magdalen," 1640
National Gallery of Art, Washington, DC

See website: *www.LuigiJannuzzi.com*
for pictures and links.

OH, THOSE ANTIQUITIES!

CAST

(In Order Of Appearance)

QUEEN

RA

CUSTOMER

AGENT

OH, THOSE ANTIQUITIES! Also won a Off-off Broadway
Award for best play from OOBR.com

OH, THOSE ANTIQUITIES! was first produced by The Peddie Players at The Peddie School in Hightstown, NJ in July 2005. The play was directed by Michael Gallagher; produced by Robert Rund; set design by John Lucs; lighting design by Marilyn Anker; Crew and Advisors: Lynn Schreffler, Robert Gargiullo & Roby McClellan. The cast was as follows:

QUEEN	Judith Ferszt
RA	Shan Raju
CUSTOMER	Edgard Garcia
AGENT	Todd Gregoire

It was presented by the Metropolitan Theatre Company at New Jersey Repertory Company, Long Branch, NJ in July 2005. The play was directed by Luigi Jannuzzi; Executive producer Gabor Barabas; Artistic Director Suzanne Barabas. The cast was as follows:

QUEEN	Stephanie Dorian
RA	Ben Masur
CUSTOMER	Joseph Franchini
AGENT	Marc Geller

It was produced by The Metropolitan Theatre Company in New York City as a selection of The Midtown International Theatre Festival, at the Workshop Theatre Main Stage, 312 West 36th St, 4th Floor, on July 2007. Executive Producer John Chatterton; Managing Director Emileena Pedigo; Artistic Director Glory Sims Bowen; Marketing Director Bob Ost. The play was directed by Elizabeth Rothan; Assistant directed by Lauren Embrey; produced by Luigi Jannuzzi/Elizabeth Rothan; lighting design by

Alan Kanevsky; projection by Eric Christopher Hoelle. The cast was as follows:

QUEEN ....Dawn E. McGee

RA ....Bruce Edward Barton

CUSTOMER ....Peter Stoll

AGENT ....Charles F. Wagner IV

(Lights rise on two Egyptians Mummies either standing side by side like the statue with His arm around **HER**, or standing 2 feet away from each other, or standing in 2 wooden boxes. **THEY** should be in white sheets with Their faces showing. The **QUEEN** calls to **RA**.)

QUEEN. Psst. (*Pause*) Psst. (*Pause*) Hey, Ra? (*Pause*) Ra, I'm talking to you. (*Pause*) I know you hear me.

(**RA** *turns back on* **QUEEN**.)

Don't turn your back on me.

(**RA** *motions to leave* **HIM** *alone*.)

Wake up. This is important.

(**RA** *turns*.)

RA. What?

QUEEN. This is an important day.

RA. Oh please.

QUEEN. And when he gets here, there're three things I want you to tell him.

RA. You tell him.

QUEEN. I am the Queen!

RA. This is getting old quick.

QUEEN. He is a common man.

RA. He's in charge of where we go. You're a sack of bones in a box. Live with it.

QUEEN. That's very mean.

65

RA. It's very true.

QUEEN. You're getting meaner every year.

RA. Cause I'm on tour with you.

QUEEN. Now number One: no college tours.

RA. That's where I'm going.

QUEEN. No we're not.

RA. It's good money.

QUEEN. It's demeaning.

RA. I like people. There're a lot of people.

QUEEN. They fog up my glass.

RA. Especially college girls.

QUEEN. Ra, you're six thousand years old and embalmed.

RA. I can look.

QUEEN. And every college wants a clipping for their lab.

RA. What's a sample?

QUEEN. They don't do that to musicians.

RA. We're different.

QUEEN. Comedians don't give scrapings.

RA. It's part of our charm.

QUEEN. We keep this up, we'll disappear.

RA. They've never taken more than a 16th of an inch.

QUEEN. At that one Florida college that nerdy looking guy took two strands of hair.

RA. Our agent left the room. What can I say?

QUEEN. Say, "No more tours."

RA. Has it ever happened before or since?

QUEEN. Two: Ask him how many frequent flyer miles we have, and get the exact figure, of what we need to get back to Egypt.

RA. I'm not going back.

QUEEN. You're going back.

RA. No.

QUEEN. I say you're going back.

RA. Say all you want.

QUEEN. You're deserting me?

RA. I'm not deserting you. You're welcome to come with me and bitch all you want.

QUEEN. Customer!

(**BOTH** *resume the pose.*) *crossed on chest.*)

(**CUSTOMER** *enters whistling, over to* **RA.**)

CUSTOMER. So you use to be the king of Egypt. Look at you now, you're in a vacuum.

(**CUSTOMER** *over to* **QUEEN.**)

Hey Queenie baby, what's happenin?

(**CUSTOMER** *leans over and puckers* **HIS** *lips three times.*)

Little kissie for the 21st century?

(*Laughs.*)

You're looking good, babe.

(**CUSTOMER** *crosses to exit.*)

For a rock!

(**CUSTOMER** *exits. Pause.*)

QUEEN. Jerk!

(**RA** *turns.*)

RA. Okay. Frequent flyer miles, what we need to get back to Egypt?

QUEEN. How come they always pick on me?

RA. They don't.

QUEEN. They do.

RA. Comes with the territory.

QUEEN. They never say anything to you.

RA. He just did.

QUEEN. Oh please.

RA. He said I'm in a vacuum.

QUEEN. He called me a rock!

RA. These are people who scream at athletes.

QUEEN. I'm not an athlete.

RA. They're a little closer.

QUEEN. And that (*Puckers lips 3 times.*) "Welcome to the 21st Century." He would never do that to you.

RA. It's because they love me.

QUEEN. They do.

RA. And they hate you.

QUEEN. It's this whole chauvinistic "KING" thing.

RA. Oh my God.

QUEEN. And who's the bimbo entombed with him?

RA. Okay, are you going to tell me number three before he gets here, or can I go back to sleep?

QUEEN. They treat me like a slave girl who slept her way to the throne.

RA. Well that's what you are.

(**RA** *resumes pose.*)

I'm going to sleep.

QUEEN. You think they know that?

RA. No.

QUEEN. I think they know that.

RA. The only ones who know that are dust, and a couple preserved cats. (*Pause.*) And I hope number three isn't you want your stuffed cats. I'm allergic, that's final.

QUEEN. I just feel like they know it and they hate me, they hate me even more now than ever.

RA. Go to sleep.

QUEEN. And number three is: I want a face-lift. (*Pause.*) Did you hear what I said? (*Pause.*) Ra? Did you hear what I said?

(**RA** *holding head.*)

RA. Will this never end?

QUEEN. I want a face-lift.

RA. Mummies don't get face-lifts.

QUEEN. Paintings get cleaned, sculptures polished, I don't see why not.

RA. I've never heard of it.

QUEEN. I want my eyes larger, and this whole sagging thing, up.

(*Pushing face up with hands*)

See how I'd look? (**PAUSE.**) Ra, look. Will you look?

(**RA** *looks, smiles.*)

I'd be pretty again.

RA. I'll ask.

QUEEN. Don't ask. Demand. You're king!

RA. I'll ask firmly.

QUEEN. Customer!

> (**THEY** *resume pose.*) **AGENT** *enter.*)

AGENT. Be not alarmed my precious. Just me.

> (**RA** *sits up.*)

RA. It's Rick.

AGENT. Let me lock these doors. There we go.

RA. Good to see you, Rick

> (**RICK** *the* **AGENT** *crosses to other side of stage.*)

AGENT. Let me lock these. There we are.

RA. You're looking good, Rick.

> (**RICK** *crosses to* **RA.**)

AGENT. Thank you. So are you both.

RA. Before we start though, there are a few things I want to mention.

AGENT. Well that's what our yearly meeting's for. Tell me your dreams, regrets, I'll tell you mine.

RA. We only have two.

> (**QUEEN** *holds up three fingers.*)

AGENT. All right.

RA. Actually, three.

AGENT. Very good. Though before that, I think I should tell you,... that you have absolutely no advanced bookings for next year.

(**THEY** *are shocked.*)

RA & QUEEN. WHAT?

AGENT. None.

RA. That's impossible.

AGENT. The British museum and the Egyptian government, just unearthed, in the Valley of the Kings: "The Tomb Of The Preserved Cats."

RA. So?

AGENT. Least that's what they're calling it.

RA. What's that have to do with us?

AGENT. Thousands of them. Different breeds, adorned in gold, diamonds, lapis lazuli, ruby, pearl eyes.

RA. So who wants to see cats?

AGENT. Everyone.

RA. Everyone wants to see cats?

AGENT. They're sold out.

RA. I can't believe it.

AGENT. Every tour, every day.

RA. Four legged creatures?

AGENT. Meow. The money's flying.

RA. I hate cats.

AGENT. They've given some of them names.

RA. No.

AGENT. Different lights on them. It's a big production. They have toys, handbags.

RA. But what about us?

QUEEN. He's the King.

AGENT. What can I tell you?

QUEEN. I'm the Queen.

AGENT. Cats are in.

RA. We've worked hard to get to this spot.

AGENT. Maybe next year, Kings are in.

RA. Rick, what about small museums?

AGENT. None.

RA. Universities?

AGENT. None.

RA. Colleges? Small colleges? Tiny southern women's schools?

AGENT. There are so many cats, they've taken individual ones, broken them off for those tours. So there are no more tours. There's nothing. In your field of art this year,... people, all the people in the world, only want to see cats.

RA. That's a very frightening concept.

AGENT. Which leaves us with one solution.

QUEEN. Oh no.

RA. Not storage.

AGENT. No.

QUEEN. Remember when you found us in that vault, we were filthy.

RA. The dust.

QUEEN. We were hidden.

RA. The odors.

QUEEN. You can't desert us, Rick.

AGENT. I'm not deserting you, you're not going to storage, cause I have a tremendous tour for you.

RA. I thought there weren't any tours?

AGENT. There aren't.

RA. Then how're we going on one?

AGENT. Cause you're going to be the King and Queen of our 200 college and university "TOMB OF THE PRESERVED CAT" tour?

RA. NO!

QUEEN. YES!

AGENT. Is that a yes or a no?

QUEEN. YES!

RA. I hate cats.

AGENT. Ra, I know

RA. I'm allergic.

AGENT. I understand.

RA. It's in our contract.

AGENT. Ra, read my lips: It's all I have.

(**RA** *is distraught.*)

RA. Oh my God.

AGENT. I'm stepping out, you two talk,...but I need an answer when I come back.

(**AGENT** *exits.*)

RA. I won't be able to breathe.

QUEEN. It's sneezing or a vault.

RA. They're going to place them all around us.

QUEEN. That or darkness.

RA. The fur gets in my nose.

QUEEN. Or no life, no sound.

RA. We're secondary to felines.

QUEEN. God knows when someone will find us down there, Ra.

RA. It's torture.

QUEEN. It's a life.

RA. It's itchy.

QUEEN. Scratch it.

RA. Very itchy.

QUEEN. You get to see college girls.

RA. I get rashes.

(**AGENT** *rushes in holding phone.*)

AGENT. Uh,...I just got a call from a Sphinx I represent, I gotta go. And I need an answer.

RA. How many cats?

AGENT. Twelve thousand eight hundred and fifty two.

RA. That's a lot of cats.

QUEEN. We'll take it.

AGENT. This time tomorrow, I'm back with the contract, meet you here,...but then where're you going, huh?

(**AGENT** *laughs, exits.*)

(**RA** *resumes pose.*)

QUEEN. You know whose cats they are, don't you?

RA. My brother Bubastite.

QUEEN. I told you to give him a job at the palace.

RA. It's always my fault.

QUEEN. "No, I don't trust him. Let's send him to that delta town of Bubastis."

RA. Everything's my fault.

QUEEN. He gets involved with that Cat Goddess Bastet.

RA. Now there was a gorgeous woman.

QUEEN. He built her that temple.

RA. Women like that deserve temples.

QUEEN. They're having annual festivals, burying mummified cats in large cemeteries.

RA. She even looked like a cat.

QUEEN. Well, I hope you're satisfied.

RA. Yeah, anything that goes wrong in history it's my fault. You can trace it right back to me.

QUEEN. A lot of it you can.

RA. Let me get some sleep.

QUEEN. And who's getting the last laugh? He is.

RA. Ha ha.

QUEEN. What goes around, comes around.

RA. I'm sleeping.

QUEEN. Ra, wake up, I have something else to tell you.

(**RA** *motions with* **HIS** *hand to go away.*)

Ra, listen to me.

(**RA** *turns back on* **QUEEN**.)

Don't turn your back on me. Wake up. This is important.

(*Lights begin to fade.*)

Psst.

(*Pause*)

Psst.

(*Pause*)

Hey, Ra?

(*Pause*)

Ra, I'm talking to you.

(*Blackout*)

COSTUMES

A small black hair piece & toga is all that is needed for each. When the AGENT comes in and doors are locked, they can move around freely.

PRODUCTION NOTE

Actors faces must be seen. The scene will not work if they are wrapped up like mummies.

Bastet is an Egyptian goddess, the cat her venerated animal. Bastet did have an annual festival with cats buried at that delta town.

The Met Museum has 13 musmmies.

Exhibits at the Metropolitan Museum of Art in New York
that corresponds to the scene:
OH, THOSE ANTIQUITIES!

"Coffin for a Sacred Cat"
Ptolemaic Period, ca 305-30 B.C.

"Memisabu and His Wife"
Dynasty 5, ca. 2350 B.C.

Outer Coffin of Henettawy"
Dynasty 21, ca. 1040-991 B.C.

"Cosmetic Cat Vessel"
Dynasty 12, ca. 1991-1783 B.C.

See website: *www.LuigiJannuzzi.com*
for pictures and links.

THE CURATOR

THE CURATOR was first produced by The Peddie Players at The Peddie School in Hightstown, NJ in July 2005. The play was directed by Michael Gallagher; produced by Robert Rund; set design by John Lucs; lighting design by Marilyn Anker; Crew and Advisors: Lynn Schreffler, Robert Gargiullo & Roby McClellan. The cast was as follows:

CURATOR....................................Tom Stevenson

MESSENGER ....Dennis Jaybendy

It was presented by the Metropolitan Theatre Company at New Jersey Repertory Company, Long Branch, NJ in July 2005. The play was directed by Luigi Jannuzzi; Executive producer Gabor Barabas; Artistic Director Suzanne Barabas. The cast was as follows:

CURATOR....................................Joseph Franchini

MESSENGER ....Liz Zazzi

It was produced by The Metropolitan Theatre Company in New York City as a selection of The Midtown International Theatre Festival, at the Workshop Theatre Main Stage, 312 West 36th St, 4th Floor, on July 2007. Executive Producer John Chatterton; Managing Director Emileena Pedigo; Artistic Director Glory Sims Bowen; Marketing Director Bob Ost. The play was directed by Elizabeth Rothan; Assistant directed by Lauren Embrey; produced by Luigi Jannuzzi/Elizabeth Rothan; lighting design by Alan Kanevsky; projection by Eric Christopher Hoelle. The cast was as follows:

CURATOR....................................Charles F. Wagner IV

SILENT GUARD ....Peter Stoll

MESSENGER ....Perryn Pomatto

Hello. You are probably wondering why I have called all of you museum guards here today. As curator of this museum I have never had to do this. And I thank you for leaving your homes for this, the worst emergency in our history. Let me cut right to the catastrophe. The painting of George Seurat's STUDY FOR SUNDAY AFTERNOON ON THE ISLAND OF LA GRANDE JATTE has escaped! The entire painting's population exited the frame around 3 am this morning. Our night security video, filmed them exiting using a makeshift ladder from the roof garden. Men, women, children, dogs, a monkey, they're all gone. A few umbrellas were found in the hedges outside the museum. Two picnic baskets filled with homemade lock picking devices and cutting tools were abandoned about a block away. It seems they used the sails from one of the boats on the water to make the ladder. Never the less, they're gone. And it's going to be rough finding them. What we are going to do is form into groups of three, each will have a specific zone around the city. Remember, they've probably split up. They could be anywhere. Remember if you do see one of them, they will appear very clear at a distance, but when you rush them, up close, they're gone. They disappear. This is pointillism. This is why in your packets you will find two tone,

red lens glasses to wear that may aid you in forming a
closer hue. Let me warn you, they don't work very well.
But that's only half of our disaster. Another painting
escaped with them. Jean Baptiste Pater's THE FAIR AT
BEZONS. It is of a troupe of actors dancing at a fair.
These are jesters, clowns, a motley crew. Also with these
actors in question, the entire village watching them is
gone. We estimate more than two hundred characters.
This is the largest break out in our history, far topping
last summer's fiasco of Paul Cezanne's THE CARD
PLAYERS which we easily located and captured on the
Coney Island rollercoaster. (*Pause.*) Today we are talking more than two hundred and fifty people. You have
copies of the pictures, blown up flash cards of each
character, a cell phone. My friends, I remember one
of my first assignments as a guard during one of these
breaks. It was an escape of the young innocent man
and the four gypsies from Georges De La Tour's THE
FORTUNE TELLER. Which was exceedingly tricky
because they were exceedingly good at doing exactly
what they are doing in the painting. Picking pockets.
They escaped in the morning rush hour. They walked
right down Fifth Avenue, with the frame, dressed in
seventeenth century clothes. They made it to Washington Square Park, Greenwich village, blended right in.
And they had a lot of money when we found them.
And guess where we found them? They were watching
a matinee of THE FANTASTIKS. To this day, when I
walk by, they all start humming, "Try to remember."
(*Pause.*) My point is, they could be anywhere. Airports,
subways, hitchhiking. Some last minute comments.
One: If you've heard any other piece talking about
this today. Word spread like vandalism. Please let me

know. Two: No comment to the media. Not that they'd believe us or are interested in our gallery meltdowns. Three: I would like to personally commend the seven guards who will be featured in this months newsletter for cracking the smuggling ring of contraband pencils and paints run by the drawings and paintings that were trying to complete themselves. I commend you for noticing the new brush strokes. Those drawings and painting in question are at the lab, they will be restored. And finally, four: Good luck guards, remember they stand out, they're only two dimensional, and right now though they feel excited to be out and wandering, soon, they'll realize their purpose in life, they'll start to panic, and they only need to see you, so keep visible, they'll run right up to you and plead to return to their canvas. It's part of their nature. It's like one curator once put it, "It's like us swimming in water, it's fun, but we know we don't belong, and soon it becomes very evident we must return where it's safe."

(**CURATOR'S** *phone rings and* **HE** *answers it, or a* **MESSENGER** *approaches* **CURATOR**. *and whispers in* **CURATOR'S** *ear.*

CURATOR *is shocked.*)

OH my God!

(**CURATOR** *closes phone or* **MESSENGER** *nods & exits.* **CURATOR** *takes deep breath, faces audience.*)

Guards. I have some shocking, though comforting news. Both paintings and all of the characters have been located. They were all arrested an hour ago, after they ran up quite a tab for lunch, at the restaurant

Sardi's, tried to pay with Seventeenth Century, two
dimensional money and the Matri'di called the police.
He said, "They looked a little sketchy." (*Pause.*) And
as we speak, they are being debriefed, and from there
they will have a short residency in the home for way-
ward paintings.

So with that news, there is only one thing left to say,
and that is at least we've had a peaceful resolution,
to this, our most serious dilemma to date. Thank you
officers.

(*Blackout.*)

COSTUMES

Guards wear blue blazers, white shirt, maroon tie, blue pants & black shoes.

PROPS

Map of Manhattan, goofy 3 D glasses, cell phone.

Exhibits at the Metropolitan Museum of Art in New York
that corresponds to the scene:
THE CURATOR

Georges Seurat
"Study for 'A Sunday on La Grande Jatte'" 1884

Jean Baptiste Pater
"The Fair at Bezons" 1733

Paul Cezanne
"The Card Players" 1890

Georges De La Tour
"The Fortune Teller" 1630's

(All are mentioned in scene.)
See website: *www.LuigiJannuzzi.com*
for pictures and links.

FERTILITY GOD FUGUE

CAST

(In Order Of Appearance)
4 or 5 ACTORS & ACTRESSES POSED
AS FERTILITY GODS WITH
PERCUSSION INSTRUMENTS

FERTILITY GOD FUGUE was first produced by The Peddie Players at The Peddie School in Hightstown, NJ in July 2005. The play was directed by Michael Gallagher; produced by Robert Rund; set design by John Lucs; lighting design by Marilyn Anker; Crew and Advisors: Lynn Schreffler, Robert Gargiullo & Roby McClellan. The cast was as follows:

GUARD ....James Caran

FERTILITY GOD ORCHESTRA ....Laura Jackson Novia
          Catherine Rowe
          Edgard Garcia
          Dennis Jaybendy

It was presented by the Metropolitan Theatre Company at New Jersey Repertory Company, Long Branch, NJ in July 2005. The play was directed by Luigi Jannuzzi; Executive producer Gabor Barabas; Artistic Director Suzanne Barabas. The cast was as follows:

GUARD ....Marc Geller

FERTILITY GOD ORCHESTRA ....Robin Marie Thomas
          Liz Zazzi
          Joseph Franchini
          Ben Masur
          Stephanie Dorian

It was produced by The Metropolitan Theatre Company in New York City as a selection of The Midtown International Theatre Festival, at the Workshop Theatre Main Stage, 312 West 36th St, 4th Floor, on July 2007. Executive Producer John Chatterton; Managing Director Emileena Pedigo; Artistic Director Glory Sims Bowen; Marketing Director Bob Ost. The play was directed by Elizabeth

Rothan; Assistant directed by Lauren Embrey; produced by
Luigi Jannuzzi/Elizabeth Rothan; lighting design by Alan
Kanevsky; projection by Eric Christopher Hoelle. Dance
Instruction by Lindsey Harwell. The cast was as follows:

GUARD ....Peter Stoll

FERTILITY GOD ORCHESTRA ....Bruce Edward Barton
                                   Emily Beatty
                                   Dustin C. Burrell
                                   Dawn E. McGee
                                   Perryn Pomatto
                                   Kristin Carter
                                   Billy Lane
                                   Lauren Embrey

(*Lights rise on 4 or 5 Fertility God statues in various poses. Fertility Gods are actors and actresses wearing masks, costumes, and holding percussion instruments: maracas, drums, finger cymbals, wood blocks, and one playing a bass like string instrument.*)

(**GUARD** *enters talking on phone.*)

GUARD. Okay, okay, I know. Do we have to decide this tonight? Why do we have to decide this tonight?

(*Pause.*)

I just thought if we're going to Italy in four months, do you want to travel 4 months pregnant? What about morning sickness? Wouldn't it be better if we wait till we get back?

(*Pause.*)

Hello? Hello?

(*Puts phone down, begins to read newspaper.*)

(*One figure begins playing, then another in a syncopated beat till four are playing excluding bass player. They play.*)

(**GUARD** *folds paper & stands. All* **GODS** *freeze, return to pose.* **GUARD** *looks around, sits, takes out telephone, dials.*)

(*Into phone.*)

Cynthia, listen. I want to start a family too. But I just think....

(*Pause.*)

Cynthia, you're overreacting.

GUARD (*Continued.*) (*Pause.*)

Yes I hear your biological clock.

(*Pause.*)

No, I'm not being sarcastic. Hello? Hello?

(*Puts phone away. Takes out pencil for crossword puzzle in paper, sits.*)

(**GODS** *begin one at a time again and this time bass player joins in last and all* **GODS** *begin to gyrate, then dance in unison with overriding bass beat. They play.*)

(**GUARD** *drops pencil.* **GODS** *freeze.* **GUARD** *stands, picks up pencil.* **GUARD** *glances around as if hearing something, then takes out phone again.*)

(*Into phone.*)

Cynthia, honey, listen to me. Just listen to me for a second?

(*Pause.*)

Really?

(*Pause.*)

Say,...say that again, what are you wearing?

(*Pause.*)

Wow!

(*Pause,* **ALL FERTILITY GODS** *sigh.*)

Cynthia, come on this isn't fair. You know I took off three times last week early, I can't.

(**GODS** *begin again.*)

No, don't talk like that, I can't. I can't.

(*Pause.* **GUARD** *smiles.*)

I,...can maybe get off an hour early.

(*Bass begins.*)

I've used just about every excuse known to man.

(**SINGER** *begins lyrics.*)

FERTILITY GOD. I want to make the beast.

GUARD. Cynthia, listen.

FERTILITY GOD. With two backs.

GUARD. You're not really wearing that, are you?

FERTILITY GOD. I want to have a baby,

GUARD. Uh,...gosh it's getting hot in here.

FERTILITY GOD. baby.

GUARD. Cynthia, maybe I can tell him that I'm sick.

FERTILITY GOD. I want to do,

GUARD. I mean, I just got over being sick.

FERTILITY GOD. What you want to do too,

GUARD. So it sounds.

FERTILITY GOD. Me.

GUARD. Cynthia don't whisper like that.

FERTILITY GOD. You want to do,

GUARD. It makes me

FERTILITY GOD. What I want to do too,

GUARD. Crazy!

FERTILITY GOD. You.

GUARD. Honey, I'll call you right back. I think I hear something.

(**GUARD** *closes phone.* **GODS** *freeze.* **GUARD** *looks around, then takes out phone and dials.*)

Honey, I just had this overwhelming feeling that maybe this trip to Italy isn't as important as starting a family.

(*Pause.*)

Well, that's what I was thinking too.

(*Pause.*)

Really? I'll be right home.

(**GUARD** *puts phone away.*)

I hope I know what I'm doing. I think I know what I'm doing.

(**GUARD** *exits. Lights begin to fade.* **FERTILITY GODS** *break into frenzy and play. Then freeze.* *Blackout.*)

INTERMISSION

COSTUMES

GUARDS wear Blue blazer, white shirt, maroon tie, blue pants & black shoes.

FERTILITY GOD: From just black leotards to full masks & costumes this scene will only work if the actors have rhythm.

PROPS

GUARD: Flashlight

FERTLITY GODS: Rhythm instruments: Maracas etc.

THE MOVEMENT:

They must be able to move to a syncopated beat that builds one instrument at a time and then breaks. (Please refrain from overt sexual moves, the comedy is in the subtle nature of the implication.) Be the Goddess.

Exhibits at the Metropolitan Museum of Art in New York
that corresponds to the scene:
FERTILITY GOD FUGUE

African-Mali-Bamana people
"Mother and Child"

African-Mali-Dogan
"Seated Couple"

See website: *www.LuigiJannuzzi.com*
for pictures and links.

THE SELF-PORTRAIT

CAST

(In Order of Appearance)

SALVATOR ROSA

THE SELF-PORTRAIT was first produced by The Peddie Players at The Peddie School in Hightstown, NJ in July 2005. The play was directed by Michael Gallagher; produced by Robert Rund; set design by John Lucs; lighting design by Marilyn Anker; Crew and Advisors: Lynn Schreffler, Robert Gargiullo & Roby McClellan. The cast was as follows:

SALVATOR ROSA ....Bruce Clough

It was presented by the Metropolitan Theatre Company at New Jersey Repertory Company, Long Branch, NJ in July 2005. The play was directed by Luigi Jannuzzi; Executive producer Gabor Barabas; Artistic Director Suzanne Barabas. The cast was as follows:

SALVATOR ROSA ....Marc Geller

It was produced by The Metropolitan Theatre Company in New York City as a selection of The Midtown International Theatre Festival, at the Workshop Theatre Main Stage, 312 West 36th St, 4th Floor, on July 2007. Executive Producer John Chatterton; Managing Director Emileena Pedigo; Artistic Director Glory Sims Bowen; Marketing Director Bob Ost. The play was directed by Elizabeth Rothan; Assistant directed by Lauren Embrey; produced by Luigi Jannuzzi/Elizabeth Rothan; lighting design by Alan Kanevsky; projection by Eric Christopher Hoelle. The cast was as follows:

SALVATOR ROSA ....Jaron Farnham

(*Lights rise on bare stage, a man dressed in black with a wreath around his head He may be carrying a book, pen and skull as he crosses the stage, stops center and addresses the audience.*)

SALVATOR ROSA. Just don't laugh. Can I ask you for that? Just don't. I know you want to,... but if you can refrain, I'd appreciate it.

(*Pause.*)

Now you're probably asking yourself, "Hey, what's the guy doing with the book and the skull and the wreath around his head?" Believe me, I've been asking myself that question for four hundred years. Because, you see, I am not only one of the artists in this museum. I am also one of the paintings in this museum. But more importantly, today, I stand before you as the new spokesperson for artists who have trapped themselves in portraits.

(*Pause.*)

I asked you not to laugh, didn't I? Didn't I? I see the smirks. I see the little upturned ends of all your mouths. I know what you're thinking. You're thinking, "You got what you deserved, buddy." Right? "You wanted to paint your own portrait? Now hang there!" That's what you're thinking, right? And you're right.

(*Pause.*)

Especially in my case. Gosh, I don't know *what* I was thinking. I was hanging around with a Philosophy professor at the University of Pisa and I thought, maybe if I paint a serious painting, people would take me seriously as a painter. So I decided to paint a meaningful, stoic philosopher contemplating existence, pondering death, and concluding in some brilliant poetic epiphany of three short words. I chose the three short words cause of the archetypical significance of three. I've always sort of been a numerologist buff a bit along with being a playwright and a poet. And then I made my big mistake, I decided, Hey... who better to be the stoic philosopher, then me. I went back and forth between should I wear a laurel branch, sort of like the Olympic runners of 776 BC, or a Cypress branch to symbolize mourning. Obviously, I decided on the cypress, the more pretentious choice. I borrowed the skull from a doctor friend. This is my book, by another stoic philosopher Seneca, and with a dark foreboding background I painted myself into the embarrassing self portrait that you can see me trapped in today. I hang in European Paintings, Central and Southern Italy. Actually I'm from Naples but lived in Rome so I'm embarrassingly right where I belong. And being trapped here for four hundred, some years, I've come to the conclusion that I'm a fine artist, but I'm a lousy thinker. I also had the idea just to hold the skull, but Nooooo, let's write on the skull too. And if you come to see me, actually my break is over in fifteen minutes, I'm lucky enough to have a curtain over my portrait that pulls down, and if you come to see me, you'll see me writing on the skull. I am writing the words, "Behold, whither, when." And I thank God everyday that I wrote it in Greek. The only salvation of pretentious writers is they write in other languages and no one understands them.

(*Pause.*)

One last item, my name is Salvator Rosa. Just in case you're looking for my painting. If you do, you can leave your card with the guard in the room and I will call you. After hours I love to talk to anyone. Especially about writing. Especially about writing about writing, painting about painting. Specifically, about the contemplation of the art and artist as one, as "THE TRAPPED ASCETIC", as so many of us like to call ourselves, and how we can deal with this, how we must deal with this. Also on behalf of the other portraits, we have just received a grant here from the Geraldine R. Dodge Foundation* to form a support group. We meet every Thursday in the Costume Institute, the only place devoid of portraits. Personally, I run the group. Personally, I need the group. So if you are a portrait, whether painted by someone else or yourself, or you are contemplating painting a portrait of someone else, or worst case scenario, OF YOURSELF. You need to hear what I, what WE have to say. Cause, my friend, take it from "A TRAPPED ASCETIC." It ain't fun!

(**HE** *holds out skull.*)

"Behold, Whither, When."

(**HE** *takes back skull, shakes head.*)

Oh my God, what was I thinking?

(**HE** *exits, lights fade.*)

---

* Or put in any local supporting foundation.

PROPS

Long black wig. Optional: skull, pen, book.

(One production has Rosa on break so he was crossing with a café'latte (coffee with milk).

COSTUME

White shirt, Black jacket

Exhibits at the Metropolitan Museum of Art in New York
that corresponds to the scene:

THE SELF PORTRAIT

Salvator Rosa 1615 - 1673
Self Portrait

See website: *www.LuigiJannuzzi.com*
for pictures and links.

HANGING WITH THE TAPESTRIES

CAST

(In Order Of Appearance)

TAPESTRIES: **BIRTH** = An Actress

LOUIS XIV as AIR = An Actor

GREENERY = An Actor

PEOPLE: **DORIS** (or **DORIAN**)

SHARON.

HANGING WITH THE TAPESTRIES was first produced by The Peddie Players at The Peddie School in Hightstown, NJ in July 2005. The play was directed by Michael Gallagher; produced by Robert Rund; set design by John Lucs; lighting design by Marilyn Anker; Crew and Advisors: Lynn Schreffler, Robert Gargiullo & Roby McClellan. The cast was as follows:

> **BIRTH** ....Judith Ferszt
>
> **LOUIS XIV as AIR**........................Todd Gregoire
>
> **GREENERY** ....Shan Raju
>
> **DORIS** ....Laura Jackson Novia
>
> **SHARON**....................................Bonnie Powell

It was presented by the Metropolitan Theatre Company at New Jersey Repertory Company, Long Branch, NJ in July 2005. The play was directed by Luigi Jannuzzi; Executive producer Gabor Barabas; Artistic Director Suzanne Barabas. The cast was as follows:

> **BIRTH** ....Stephanie Dorian
>
> **LOUIS XIV as AIR**........................Joseph Franchini
>
> **GREENERY** ....Marc Geller
>
> **DORIS** ....Liz Zazzi
>
> **SHARON**....................................Robin Marie Thomas

It was produced by The Metropolitan Theatre Company in New York City as a selection of The Midtown International Theatre Festival, at the Workshop Theatre Main Stage, 312 West 36th St, 4th Floor, on July 2007. Executive Producer John Chatterton; Managing Director Emileena Pedigo; Artistic Director Glory Sims Bowen; Marketing Director Bob Ost. The play was directed by Elizabeth

Rothan; Assistant directed by Lauren Embrey; produced by Luigi Jannuzzi/Elizabeth Rothan; lighting design by Alan Kanevsky; projection by Eric Christopher Hoelle. The cast was as follows:

BIRTH	Emily Beatty
LOUIS XIV as AIR	Dustin C. Burrell
GREENERY	Billy Lane
DORIS	(Dorian as a Male) Perryn Pomatto
SHARON	Kristin Carter

(*Lights rise on three sleeping actors standing next to each other left center, center and right center stage. They can also be on small ladders. The first actor (*BIRTH*) yawns and wakes up suddenly.*)

BIRTH. Whoa! (*Pause.*) Hey, the museum's open! (*Pause.*) Louie, wake up!

LOUIE (*Yawns.*)

BIRTH. How could all three of us oversleep?

LOUIE. (*With French Accent*) What?

BIRTH. Louie, regain consciousness!

LOUIE. Gosh it's light.

BIRTH. Wake Greenery up. They're going to be here any second.

LOUIE. I don't think we should wake him till we know what we're doing.

BIRTH. It's too late. They said Ten. By the shadows it's Ten.

LOUIE. Greenery, Greenery!

BIRTH. This is going to be a fiasco.

LOUIE. Greenery!

GREENERY. (*Yawns.*)

BIRTH. No wonder they're so successful, we're so lethargic.

GREENERY. What time is it?

LOUIE. They're almost here.

BIRTH. Greenery, get up, they said they're coming for you today.

115

GREENERY. I can't believe they'd pick on me.

LOUIE. Believe it.

GREENERY. They've never tried a tapestry.

BIRTH. That's what the paintings thought. Now, they go in and out of them like doors.

LOUIE. Not all of them.

BIRTH. Not all, but some are sitting ducks.

LOUIE. The poor Monet's.

BIRTH. Oh, what they've done to the Monet's.

LOUIE. One character in Monet's "La Grenouillere" told me that one of these women spent a week there swimming, dining.

BIRTH. Can you imagine?

GREENERY. The nerve.

BIRTH. In Monet's "Garden at Sainte-Adresse" they took a boat out.

GREENERY. Disgusting.

LOUIE. In Canaletto's, "Piazza San Marco"? Every Wednesday, second cafe from the bell tower, they have cappuccino.

GREENERY. Okay, I'm scared.

LOUIE. You should be.

GREENERY. How do I stop them?

BIRTH. I have no idea.

LOUIE. Well, I have spoken to a lot of paintings *that have* repelled them.

GREENERY. How'd *they* do it?

LOUIE. For instance, you don't see them picking on the Biblical ones like you, "The Birth Of The Virgin."

BIRTH. I wouldn't think so.

LOUIE. I mean let's say they pick you, they pick "The Birth of the Virgin," what is going to happen when they arrive?

BIRTH. Saint Ann, One of my 12 handmaidens, maybe even Mary, would throw them out.

LOUIE. They're going to tell them "bye bye."

BIRTH. Plus I'm a biblical painting, I'm blessed.

LOUIE. Of course. Cause some artists, yours is a good example, have insured their paintings against attack cause the very fabric of their metaphor goes against the possibility of access.

GREENERY. Some of us are just lucky.

LOUIE. Most biblical scenes are.

GREENERY. But how is this helping me?

LOUIE. See, my instinct is, we have to think of some reason for you to focus on, to close the fabric of your very being, just as these Biblical ones have.

GREENERY. I'm a forest scene. I have no people to repulse them.

LOUIE. It's in the fabric of your being, not your characters.

BIRTH. Louie has something here. There are paintings they don't consider cause they're so repulsive, that's what we have to aim for.

LOUIE. Like Henri Rousseau's "The Repast of the Lion."

GREENERY. Well, of course they're not going in there.

BIRTH. Louie, it's a jungle, it's a lion eating a Jaguar.

GREENERY. They'd be lunch.

LOUIE. Nick Poussin's "The Abduction Of The Sabine Women." You don't see them vacationing there.

BIRTH. Louie, we're getting off the subject.

LOUIE. No, I don't think so, cause, you see, what these pieces have is a back story.

GREENERY. A what?

LOUIE. You want to repulse these two?

GREENERY. Yes.

LOUIE. You want to close your fabric to their very being?

GREENERY. Yes.

LOUIE. Cause like "Birth" says, you allow these two in your forest.

GREENERY. Oh God no.

LOUIE. They're walking around, petting your deer, feeding your birds.

GREENERY. I think I'm going to get sick.

LOUIE. They go in your woods, set up a tent.

GREENERY. Don't even go there.

LOUIE. You might never get them out.

BIRTH. Louie, you're scaring him.

LOUIE. He needs to be scared.

BIRTH. He needs to focus. How does he focus?

LOUIE. Do you know why they never pick on me? Cause I am the king. I am the King of France. I, my mistress, our six kids commemorated here, in this tapestry, made by nuns, blessed by nuns, will have these two biddies for lunch. They'd think "The Repast Of The Lion" was a picnic.

(*Two ladies enter,* **THEY** *are Dressed like librarians. Each carries an open catalog.*)

DORIS. This is the room, Sharon.

SHARON. Oh yes.

BIRTH. They're here!

GREENERY. Oh no, it's them.

DORIS. "Greenery," that's it.

LOUIE. Don't panic.

GREENERY. What do I do, Louie?

SHARON. Oh, it's beautiful.

LOUIE. Do not panic.

GREENERY. Tell me what to do.

LOUIE. You need a back-story.

DORIS. Very peaceful.

SHARON. Calming.

GREENERY. I have no back-story.

LOUIE. Oh yes you do.

DORIS. A lot of places to hide.

DORIS & SHARON. (**BOTH WOMEN** *giggle.*)

LOUIE. You are a tapestry commemorating trees: A Pear, Chestnut, Oak! Pear is for?

GREENERY. Printing blocks!

LOUIE. Chestnut for?

BIRTH. Rafters.

LOUIE. And Oak for building boats! Your back story is INDUSTRY! Focus on that! Men harvesting your trees.

DORIS. Do you want to go in first?

SHARON. That's fine with me.

(**SHARON** *sits and begins deep breathing with eyes shut.*)

LOUIE. Focus on these men from the wood industry!

BIRTH. Oh yes, BIG men!

(**LOUIE** *reacts mildly to* **BIRTH.**)

DORIS. (**DORIS** *is massaging Sharon's shoulders.*)
    Now concentrate, Sharon.

LOUIE. Concentrate on the BIG men.

BIRTH. Big, SWEATY men!

GREENERY. Huh?

LOUIE. Just focus.

> (**DORIS** *could dangle a swinging pendulum before*
> **SHARON.**)

DORIS. Focus and concentrate.

GREENERY. But I'm a beautiful forest!

LOUIE. No, you're a dismal picture of the wood industry.

BIRTH. Just focus on those big, sweaty, drunken men with
    long handle axes and

LOUIE. Yes, THANK YOU, Birth!

DORIS. Be the tapestry.

GREENERY. Oh, I get it!

SHARON. I am the tapestry.

GREENERY. I see what you mean now. I feel the fear!

LOUIE. Good! Inject that fear into your fabric.

SHARON. I am the Greenery.

DORIS. You are.

LOUIE. Translate it into a fear of penetration.

BIRTH. Oohh!

DORIS. Feel the green.

SHARON. I feel it.

LOUIE. Feel the chopping.

GREENERY. I feel it.

SHARON. I see the woodland animals.

DORIS. She sees them.

GREENERY. I see the trees falling.

BIRTH. He sees them.

DORIS. Smell the damp forest.

SHARON. Yes.

LOUIE. Smell the raging fires.

GREENERY. Yes.

DORIS. Up you go, Sharon.

LOUIE. Up she rises!

DORIS. Here you go.

GREENERY. Here she comes!

DORIS. Straight ahead.

LOUIE. Straight to where the lumberjacks are!

DORIS. Two feet.

GREENERY. The drunken lumberjacks!

DORIS. One foot.

BIRTH. Drunken, sweaty, hairy-chested, muscular.

LOUIE. That will do, Birth!

    (**SHARON** *crosses in back of* **GREENERY.** *We can not see* **SHARON. SHARON** *is now in the Tapestry.*)

SHARON. I'm in. I'm in.

BIRTH, GREENERY, LOUIE. NOOOOO!

DORIS. Yessss!

SHARON. I'm in Doris.

DORIS. We did it. We did it...

BIRTH. Oh no, Greenery.

LOUIE. Don't give up, keep it going.

GREENERY. Why?

DORIS. I knew you could do it.

GREENERY. What's the point, Louie?

DORIS. Okay, I'm coming right in.

(**DORIS** sits and begins breathing.)

LOUIE. You listen to me Greenery; you keep it going not only for your sake but for the sake of every tapestry hanging here. Now repeat: "Drunken woodsmen are closing in."

SHARON. Doris?

GREENERY. Drunken woodsmen are closing in.

DORIS. Be the tapestry.

SHARON. Doris, can you hear me, answer me?

GREENERY. Drunken woodsmen are closing in.

(**DORIS** *breaks and leans forward.*)

DORIS. Sharon, I'll be right in.

LOUIE. Drunken woodsmen with dogs.

GREENERY. Drunken woodsmen with dogs.

SHARON. Doris, wait a minute, before you come in.

DORIS. What? What is it?

LOUIE. Can you smell it?

GREENERY. I can smell it.

LOUIE. Smell the burning forest.

GREENERY. Smell the scorched earth.

SHARON. Doris, I just get a feeling it's not that idyllic.

DORIS. Why? What's wrong?

SHARON. Well, the woodland animals seem nervous. And I hear drunk men singing! There's something very wrong.

DORIS. I'm coming in.

SHARON. No, I'm coming out.

LOUIE. Watch out for that tree!

DORIS. You can't come out, you just got in.

GREENERY. (*Yells.*) TIMBERRRR!

SHARON. The entire tapestries vibrating, it's shaking.

DORIS. Then come out, come out, Sharon.

LOUIE & BIRTH. Watch out!

GREENERY. WATCH OUT EVERYONE!

> (**SHARON** *springs from behind* **GREENERY**, *throwing* **HERSELF** *on the floor in front of* **DORIS.**)

SHARON. AHHH! (*Pause.*) Oh!

> (**SHARON** *sits up.*)

Oh!

DORIS. What happened?

BIRTH. Yea!

LOUIE. You did it!

DORIS. You smell like smoke.

BIRTH. You repelled the attack.

SHARON. There's something wrong in that tapestry.

DORIS. It's so beautiful Sharon.

SHARON. I could hear drunken lumberjacks laughing, it's smokey, it's a nightmare in there.

LOUIE. Hip, hip,.. hooray!

LOUIE AND BIRTH & GREENERY. HIP, HIP,... HOORAY!

DORIS. It looks peaceful.

SHARON. Well, it's not! Believe me. I was in there!

DORIS. Hmmmmm…what you say makes sense; this is a commemoration to industry. Read this scroll about the Pear tree. "By Woodman's edge I faint and fall, by craftsman's edge I tell the tale." This Pear Tree is about to be chopped down for printing blocks.

GREENERY. (*Yawns.*) I am exhausted.

DORIS. And the trees know it.

SHARON. They're scared.

LOUIE. And ready to fall on you.

GREENERY. (*Dozing off.*) Gosh, I'm falling,...falling.

DORIS. Cause the drunk men are coming.

GREENERY. Asleep.

(**GREENERY** *is asleep.*)

BIRTH. You deserve a nap Greenery.

SHARON. We have to warn everyone not to go in this one.

BIRTH. And so do you, Louie.

DORIS. Someone could get hurt.

BIRTH. It was exhausting just to watch you guide the attack.

LOUIE. Well, we have to look out for each other.

SHARON. Gives me the shivers.

LOUIE. We have to take care of each other.

BIRTH. (*Yawns.*) I think I'm going to take a nap too.

DORIS. We really have to investigate these before we go in.

LOUIE. We have to defend one another.

SHARON. I don't want to do anymore new ones today.

(**BIRTH** *is asleep.*)

LOUIE. As the King of France I used to defend a whole nation.

DORIS. I don't blame you.

SHARON. In fact, I think we should stay away from the Tapestries in general.

LOUIE. Let alone defend my tapestry here against attacks from my wife.

DORIS. Let's go to the "Canaletto" and get a cappuccino.

LOUIE. Did I ever tell you about the time?

(**LOUIE** *notices both Tapestries are asleep.*)

SHARON. Then maybe a Monet for a swim.

LOUIE. Oh no, they're napping again.

(**DORIS** *and* **SHARON** *begin flipping though catalogue.*)

DORIS. I hear you can rent boats in most Monet's.

LOUIE. I guess I might as well take a nap too.

SHARON. That's what I hear.

LOUIE. We all deserve it.

(**LOUIE** *yawns, is drowsy.*)

DORIS. In fact, I have this week's newsletter, it lists all the paintings where you can rent boats.

SHARON. Last week's newsletter was on exotic landscape.

DORIS. Wasn't that great?

SHARON. Have you been to Frans Post's "Brazilian Landscape"?

DORIS. No.

SHARON. You have to go in there.

(*Pointing to catalogue.*)

Here it is. It's exotic,... and historical.

DORIS. Let's go.

SHARON & DORIS. Let's go now!

(**DORIS** *and* **SHARON** *nod and giggle, cross to exit.*
LOUIE *watches them till* **THEY** *exit, shakes head, takes a*
deep breath, yawns, closes eyes, and falls asleep.

LIGHT fade, Blackout.)

COSTUMES

BIRTH: White robe, scarf, slippers

GREENERY: Can be as simple as a faux vine around his neck
draping down his chest.

LOUIS XIV: A royal like robe, white shirt

DORIS: Small swinging pendulum, Purse, finger cymbals,
newsletter, binoculars, guidebook to Museum. Clothes
in productions have ranged from very conservative to
colorful/flamboyant.

SHARON: Guidebook, newsletter. Clothes have ranged from
offbeat, creative and novel to conservative. Perhaps contrast Sharon and Doris in style.

Exhibits at the Metropolitan Museum of Art in New York
that corresponds to the scene:
HANGING WITH THE TAPESTRIES

Air, 1683 a.d.
French Tapestry commemorating Louis XVI
and His mistress and their six children.

Greenery, 1905 a.d.
English Tapestry
commemorating the use of wood in Art and Industry.

Birth Of The Virgin
Florence, Italy
3rd Quarter 15th C.
(Check out the silk used for hair.)

Grenouillere, 1869
Claude Monet
(The following are mentioned in the scene.)

Garden At Sainte-Adresse, 1867
Clalude Monet

Giovanni Canaletto
Piazza San Marco, 1730

Henri-Julien-Felix Rousseau
The Repast of the Lion, ca 1907

Nicolas Poussin
The Abduction of the Sabine Women, ca 1633-34

Frans Post
A Brazilian Landscape, 1650

See website: *www.LuigiJannuzzi.com*
for pictures and links.

THE DRAWING ROOM GUARD'S BIG LIE

CAST

(In Order Of Appearance)
THE GUARD (RICHARD)

Note: If done as a female the only changes needed are:
RICHARD to **CHRISTINE**, "son" to "daughter", a few "he" to
"she" & "his" to "her", and the response, "He has talent" to
"She has talent."

THE DRAWING ROOM GUARD'S BIG LIE was first produced by The Peddie Players at The Peddie School in Hightstown, NJ in July 2005. The play was directed by Michael Gallagher; produced by Robert Rund; set design by John Lucs; lighting design by Marilyn Anker; Crew and Advisors: Lynn Schreffler, Robert Gargiullo & Roby McClellan. The cast was as follows:

GUARD ....Todd Gregoire

It was presented by the Metropolitan Theatre Company at New Jersey Repertory Company, Long Branch, NJ in July 2005. The play was directed by Luigi Jannuzzi; Executive producer Gabor Barabas; Artistic Director Suzanne Barabas. The cast was as follows:

GUARD ....Ben Masur

It was produced by The Metropolitan Theatre Company in New York City as a selection of The Midtown International Theatre Festival, at the Workshop Theatre Main Stage, 312 West 36th St, 4th Floor, on July 2007. Executive Producer John Chatterton; Managing Director Emileena Pedigo; Artistic Director Glory Sims Bowen; Marketing Director Bob Ost. The play was directed by Elizabeth Rothan; Assistant directed by Lauren Embrey; produced by Luigi Jannuzzi/Elizabeth Rothan; lighting design by Alan Kanevsky; projection by Eric Christopher Hoelle. The cast was as follows:

GUARD ....Perryn Pomatto

(*Lights rise on* **GUARD** *standing center stage but with head turned looking offstage left.*)

(**GUARD** *pauses 2 beats, turns head to look offstage right 2 beats, then looks at audience 2 beats, then* **GUARD** *turns head toward stage left.*)

GUARD. (*To off left.*) Excuse me, Sir. Please stay behind the red rope. Thank you.

(*To audience.*)

I graduated Art school with honors. I've had many drawings in many shows all over the city. My mother thinks I'm a thriving artist, I make a living off of it, I don't obviously. And that's how the problem, or what I call, "my big lie" started. When a friend of a friend, somehow told someone who told my mother that "My work is at this museum."

(**GUARD** *glances to right, reacts to off right.*)

Miss excuse me,... the taking of flash photography is not permitted. Besides that drawing has a wonderful poster and an inexpensive postcard in our gift shop. (*Pause.*) You're welcome.

(*To audience.*)

So my Mother calls and I, I don't know why,...I told my Mother that, "Yes, this museum, this monument to art has, as part of its permanent collection, one of my

135

drawings." So she's in Montana, I'm here, everything's fine. She put a story in the local paper, they called, I gave them a couple quotes. I thank God everyday it didn't go any further. And I think my Mom bought all the copies anyway. So I felt safe. Till one day, I was standing here and around that corner, on a very crowded Saturday afternoon came my Mother. I heard her ask a man, "Could you tell me where the Perantoni is." That's my name Richard Perantoni. She said, "The guard in the other room told me that the Richard Perantoni is in this room." I hid my face. My Mom started looking at one work after another. Squinting, glancing up and down with her bifocals, bragging to some patrons that her son had a drawing hanging in the museum. And that's when I got the idea, when my mind flipped to its dark side. (*Pause.*) I ran. I found my best friend Roy. Roy is a guard in the Costume Institute. Roy knew the story. Roy knew what had to be done. We went back to the room, Roy told me to wait near the door. (*Pause.*) And Roy did the deed. Roy went to my Mother, and holding out his arm, with all the charm of Judas Iscariot, he said, "Excuse me, we have been informed that you are the Mother of Richard Perantoni one of our artists." My Mother beamed. She nodded. For the first time in her life, she could not speak. Roy continued, "May I escort you to your son's masterpiece." And taking her arm, Roy escorted my Mother across the room until they stood before one of our museums greatest masterpieces: "Studies for the Libyan Sibyl." It's a sketch of a Sibyl, a prophet that the artist was using as a guide as he frescoed it onto the ceiling of THE SISTINE CHAPEL. (*Pause.*) Yes, Roy was now convincing my Mother that **I** was

Michelangelo Buonarroti of Florence Italy, 1475 to 1564. And she bought it! And she turned to a man standing next to her and said, "That's my son's." The man said, "It looks like a Michelangelo Buonarroti." To which she replied, "He has talent."

(**GUARD** *to off left.*)

Excuse me Sir, you dropped your wallet. (*Pause.*) You're welcome.

(*To audience.*)

Roy took my Mother to the cafeteria for Cappuccino and a Danish, even called her a cab. I am deeply indebted to Roy. That evening my Mother called me from her hotel. We had dinner. I listened to her story 5 times. And the next day we took a taxi together to the airport. And that's when, in the taxi ride home, I had my revelation. I came to the conclusion that I am not an artist. That I guard art. And I guard my Mother from my lack of it. That is when I realized that I have been cursed with the greatest curse of all, the curse of a little bit of talent. Enough to keep going but not enough to ever make anything happen. And I must tell you, that that ride was the lowest point of my life. Until I arrived home and there was a message on my answering machine. And the message was that the museum, this museum, has just decided to exhibit as part of their local contemporary artists wing, one of my drawings. (*Pause.*) I was stunned. I started jumping up and down. I didn't know who to call. I couldn't call my Mother. I called Roy. I said, "Roy, I got a message on my answering machine. They're going to put one of my drawings in the museum." Roy said, "So, this time, do you want to go for the Rossetti or the Leonardo Da'Vinci?" (*Pause.*) That was one month ago. And today is the first day my drawing is on exhibit. I'm sorry to bend your ear but I had to tell someone. I keep thinking someday, someone may come by and actually ask me for directions.

(*Pause.*) You would? Well sure. You go right down this corridor, take a right and in the first room, mine is the third drawing on the right. (*Pause.*) And by the way,... thank you.

(**GUARD** *stands silent looking right then left as lights fade.*)

(*Blackout.*)

COSTUMES

Guards wear blue blazers, blue pants, white shirt, maroon tie, black shoes.

Exhibits at the Metropolitan Museum of Art in New York
that corresponds to the scene:
DRAWING ROOM GUARD'S BIG LIE

Michelangelo Buonarroti
"Studies for the Libyan Sibyl" 1508 - 1512

Dante Gabriel Rossetti
"Lady Lilith," 1867

Leonardo Da Vinci
"Studies for a Nativity" 1483

(The Buonarroti is in the scene.
The DaVinci and Rossetti are mentioned.)
See website: *www.LuigiJannuzzi.com*
for pictures and links.

1-555-HELP-ART

CAST

(In Order Of Appearance)

SOCRATES
THE VOICE
CURATOR or **SECURITY GUARD**

1-555-HELP-ART was first produced by The Peddie Players at The Peddie School in Hightstown, NJ in July 2005. The play was directed by Michael Gallagher; produced by Robert Rund; set design by John Lucs; lighting design by Marilyn Anker; Crew and Advisors: Lynn Schreffler, Robert Gargiullo & Roby McClellan. The cast was as follows:

SOCRATES...................................Tom Stevenson

VOICE ....Bruce Clough

GUARD ....Edgard Garcia

It was presented by the Metropolitan Theatre Company at New Jersey Repertory Company, Long Branch, NJ in July 2005. The play was directed by Luigi Jannuzzi; Executive producer Gabor Barabas; Artistic Director Suzanne Barabas. The cast was as follows:

SOCRATES...................................Joseph Franchini

VOICE ....Robin Marie Thomas

GUARD ....Stephanie Dorian

It was produced by The Metropolitan Theatre Company in New York City as a selection of The Midtown International Theatre Festival, at the Workshop Theatre Main Stage, 312 West 36th St, 4th Floor, on July 2007. Executive Producer John Chatterton; Managing Director Emileena Pedigo; Artistic Director Glory Sims Bowen; Marketing Director Bob Ost. The play was directed by Elizabeth Rothan; Assistant directed by Lauren Embrey; produced by Luigi Jannuzzi/ Elizabeth Rothan; lighting design by Alan Kanevsky; projection by Eric Christopher Hoelle. The cast was as follows:

SOCRATES...................................Dustin C Burrell

VOICE ....Billy Lane

GUARD ....Peter Stoll

(*Enter* **SOCRATES** *in a toga pacing cautiously glancing left & right.*)

SOCRATES. Alright the lobby. I'm almost out. But where do I go from here? Now where's the cell phone that guy threw away.

(*Takes out cell phone.*)

Okay. Now where's the number that post modern nude gave me? And she made it, she hasn't been back. Got it.

(*Reads.*)

1-555-HELP-Art. That's me. I need help, refuge. I'm on the lam now. (*Pause, dials.*) One, five, five, five, H.e.l.p. ...A.R.T.

(**HE** *looks around, phone rings.*)

Okay. Great, it's ringing. Cause I'm tired of reaching for the hemlock, pontificating with my finger in the air.

(*The line answers.*)

Hello? This is Socrates from the painting, "The Death Of Socrates."

(*During the call, the voice- over is the voice on the other end of the phone.*)

VOICE. Hello.

SOCRATES. I want to switch from drinking hemlock to exile. I'm going for the exile. I mean, how bad could it be?

VOICE. You have reached the automated information system of "ART HELP," the helpful system with your personal art needs in our system. If you are calling because you are running away from your museum, press one, if you wish to return to your museum, press two.

SOCRATES. One

(HE *presses number.*)

VOICE. You have pressed two to return to your museum.

SOCRATES. No. I'm escaping.

VOICE. If you are lost inside your museum press one, outside your museum press two, being held hostage three, to return to the main menu press four.

SOCRATES. Four.

(HE *presses button.*)

VOICE. You have pressed three, held hostage.

SOCRATES. No, I wanted four. This isn't logical.

VOICE. If you are being stolen as we speak press one, already stolen press two, press three to return to the main menu.

SOCRATES. Three.

VOICE. You have pressed one, being stolen.

SOCRATES. No. Listen to me.

VOICE. If you are being stolen to make a statement press one, stolen to be sold press two, if you are being vandalized just for the hell of it press three, press four to return to the main menu.

SOCRATES. Four, four.

(**HE** *presses button.*)

VOICE. You have chosen "vandalized for the hell of it." If you are being graffittied by youth press one, ripped from your frame, two, partially shredded, three, to return to the main menu, press four.

SOCRATES. Four, four.

(*Presses button.*)

VOICE. You are being graffittied by youth.

SOCRATES. Four.

(*Presses button.*)

VOICE. You are being graffittied and ripped from your frame.

SOCRATES. No four.

(**HE** *presses again.*)

VOICE. You are being graffittied, ripped from your frame and partially shredded.

SOCRATES. What is wrong with this phone?

VOICE. If you want this call traced and help immediately sent, press one now. If you would like to hear one of our many music selections, press two, to return to the main menu press three.

SOCRATES. Three please, please.

(*Presses button.*)

VOICE. Security has been notified of your location.

SOCRATES. No Oh no.

VOICE. If while waiting you would like to hear opera press one, Grand opera, two,...madrigal, three....

SOCRATES. Why is this happening?

VOICE. Violin, four.

SOCRATES. Main menu.

(**HE** *presses button.*)

VOICE. Lyre, five. Sounds of the 1470's six. Sounds of the 1460's seven

SOCRATES. Cancel that.

(**HE** *presses button.*)

VOICE. You have selected Music of Cloistered Nuns. For Sister Bart, press one.

SOCRATES. Cancel everything.

(**HE** *presses many buttons.*)

How does this turn off? It doesn't turn off.

(**SECURITY GUARD** *or* **CURATOR** *enters onto stage.*)

SECURITY. Socrates, what are you doing?

SOCRATES. Don't come near me.

SECURITY. Hey, what do you say we talk?

SOCRATES. (*Into phone.*) Oh no you don't, Art Help.

SECURITY. Plus you're in the lobby, people are watching.

SOCRATES. (*Dialing.*) One, five, five, five, H.e.l.p. - A.R.T.

SECURITY. Socrates, like you always say,...be logical about this.

SOCRATES. (*Into phone.*) Listen, I was first exhibited at the Salon of 1787 on the eve of the French Revolution!

VOICE. Hello?

SOCRATES. (*Into Phone.*) Hello. This is Socrates, Greek philosopher, French painting, I'm in the lobby, a public place, I'm declaring asylum.

SECURITY. Socrates?

VOICE. You have reached the automated information system of "ART HELP."

SOCRATES. Listen to me!

SECURITY. Soc, put the phone down.

SOCRATES. I stand for stoical self sacrifice in a neo classical style and I demand an answer!

VOICE. The art system with your personal precepts in our system.

SECURITY. Please give me the phone.

SOCRATES. Hello? Hello?

SECURITY. Please?

SOCRATES. (*Screams into phone.*) I CAN'T TAKE IT! I CAN'T TAKE IT ANYMORE!

(**SOCRATES** *holds phone out.*)

It's starting again.

SECURITY. What is?

(**SECURITY** *takes phone, holds up to ear.*)

SOCRATES. The voice. The senseless, unending voice.

SECURITY. It's an answering system.

SOCRATES. It's inhuman, illogical.

SECURITY. A lot out there is. That's why Socrates,...

(**SECURITY** *puts arm around* **SOCRATES**.)

Socrates, buddy,... isn't this what we've been talking about? Isn't this why I said I'd stay in here if I were you? And you like it in here, don't you? You always say, everything's numbered, in the right spot.

SOCRATES. I hear all the streets are numbered in New York.

SECURITY. Oh the streets are numbered. (*Pause.*) But that's where the logic ends.

SOCRATES. What about meaning? After all, out there is what all in here, is based on.

SECURITY. Yea but in here, is all the meaning *of* out there.

SOCRATES. Is that right?

SECURITY. Of course. That's why they all come in here. They're looking for meaning and you have it, we have it.

SOCRATES. I guess you're right.

(**SECURITY** *leads* **SOCRATES** *toward offstage.*)

SECURITY. Of course I'm right.

SOCRATES. I just get confused sometimes.

SECURITY. It's understandable. But when you think logically it makes sense, doesn't it?

SOCRATES. Yea. Yea I guess it does,... thanks.

SECURITY. Don't mention it.

(*Blackout.*)

COSTUMES

SOCRATES: Toga, cell phone, sandals.

GUARD: Blue blazer, white shirt, maroon tie, blue pants &
black shoes.

Exhibits at the Metropolitan Museum of Art in New York
that corresponds to the scene:

1-555-HELP-ART

Jacques-Louis David
"The Death of Socrates" 1787

See website: *www.LuigiJannuzzi.com*
for pictures and links.

MISGUIDED TOUR

CAST

WOMAN

MISGUIDED TOUR was first produced by The Peddie Players at The Peddie School in Hightstown, NJ in July 2005. The play was directed by Michael Gallagher; produced by Robert Rund; set design by John Lucs; lighting design by Marilyn Anker; Crew and Advisors: Lynn Schreffler, Robert Gargiullo & Roby McClellan. The cast was as follows:

   WOMAN......................................Laura Jackson Novia

It was presented by the Metropolitan Theatre Company at New Jersey Repertory Company, Long Branch, NJ in July 2005. The play was directed by Luigi Jannuzzi; Executive producer Gabor Barabas; Artistic Director Suzanne Barabas. The cast was as follows:

   WOMAN......................................Robin Marie Thomas

It was produced by The Metropolitan Theatre Company in New York City as a selection of The Midtown International Theatre Festival, at the Workshop Theatre Main Stage, 312 West 36th St, 4th Floor, on July 2007. Executive Producer John Chatterton; Managing Director Emileena Pedigo; Artistic Director Glory Sims Bowen; Marketing Director Bob Ost. The play was directed by Elizabeth Rothan; Assistant directed by Lauren Embrey; produced by Luigi Jannuzzi/Elizabeth Rothan; lighting design by Alan Kanevsky; projection by Eric Christopher Hoelle. The cast was as follows:

   WOMAN......................................Jasmin Singer

(*Lights rise on a very bubbly* **WOMAN** *giving a tour to imaginary people that may or may not be there.*)

WOMAN. Good morning, good morning everyone. Please pull in a little closer, this is a little larger group than I'm accustomed to,...but if we squeeze in. Sir, if you'll squeeze. And if you'll let that lady squeeze. (*Pause.*) Oh, you are good squeezers, good. Perfect. Now if we can maintain this shape, follow me, and listen,... your personalized tour of 20th century society outcasts, evoking their miseries of poverty and despair, like Pablo Picasso's masterpiece THE BLIND MAN'S MEAL, will be a simply thrilling experience. (*Pause.*) Follow me.

(*Referring to Georgia O'Keeffe's "BLACK ABSTRACTION".*)

Who knows who this is? Anyone? Anyone? (*Pause.*) It's you, that's who this is. That is exactly what Georgia O'Keeffe meant in 1927 in New York under the effects of anesthesia, trying to reach up, to that distancing white dot of sunlight, see her arm reaching up, through the three darkening rings as she is being overwhelmed, being sucked down into the vortex of darkness. (*Pause, to tour.*) Ever feel like that? No? (*To Painting.*) See, it doesn't have to be anesthesia. It can just be that feeling you get when your rent's overdue, or your boyfriend's hitting on one of your girlfriends, or your sister's having her third baby and you can't even maintain a job. Or that,...little white dot you stare at when you lie on your bed at night,... and contemplate why you're not getting cast in anymore commercials or even have the energy to pound the pavement to get rejected. No,...you're just picking up pocket change here and there giving tours of depressing art while your whole life is spinning out of control. (*Pause. Smiles at tour.*) Ohhhhh. I love this painting. (*Pause.*) Follow me.

(*Referring to Pablo Picasso's "Gertrude Stein".*)

Gertrude Stein posed 80 times for this painting by Pablo Picasso. Many people said Stein didn't even look like the portrait. Picasso said, "She will." But see, it doesn't have to be Gertrude Stein; it can just be that feeling you get when you look upon such matriarchal, archetypal, domineering figures that I'm sure we've all had in our past.

(*To tour.*)

Haven't we? Haven't we all? (*To painting.*) Look at her, all smug, sitting there, watching soap operas while the children are locked in different rooms. All crying, "Open the door, Mommy, open the door." But she has no intentions of opening those doors. No, she just sits there eating wafer cookie after creme puff talking on the phone about hair colors. No, that one little girl, way in a back bedroom, screaming, "Let me out, Mommy, let me out",... no one can hear that poor little girl, and this woman doesn't care. (*Turns, smile to tour.*) Wow! It's quite a painting, isn't it! (*Pause.*)

Follow me.

(*Referring to Lucian Freud's "Naked Man, Back view."*)

Look at this. This is British, 1992. This is Lucian Freud's, "Naked Man, Back View." Is that disgusting, or what? It's a painting of London actor Leigh Bowery. Huge man, head shaven, a landscape of flesh beaten by gravity.

(*Pause.*)

Someone get a towel! (**SHE** *laughs and to tour.*) But see it doesn't have to be about Leigh Bowery's "naked, back view." It can just be the feeling you get when you see your own "naked, back view." (*To tour.*) Have you seen your own "naked, back view" lately? (*To another.*) Have you seen your "naked, back view?" (*To painting.*) I mean, isn't it really about time ravaging us,...all of us, little by moment, by day, by decade? My God, my breasts are sagging! My face,...I mean,...you really need money to maintain a career in entertainment there's no doubt about it. And when you're young, and chipper, and everything bounces, and every weekend you're out there schmoozing' nude with the lights on,...the world is your oyster. But when that shell closes, and you're outside sagging like poor Leigh Bowery here,... and you find the only job you can get is posing naked as a landscape O'flesh. (*Pause.*) Hey, personally, I think it's about time to hand in your equity card and head for a New Jersey pasture. (*Pause.*) My God, this painting gives me the chills, doesn't it? (*Cheerfully to tour.*) Hey, let's do another, shall we? Follow me!

(*Referring to Edward Hopper's painting "The Light-house at Two Lights."*)

This is Edward Hopper's tranquil oil scene of the lighthouse and guard outpost on the jagged point of Cape Elizabeth in Maine. Notice the sky, the wispy clouds, the feeling of isolation so prevalent in all of Hopper's work from his people to his oceanless view of this powerful geometric form.

Notice the bright light and deep shadow contrast of the morning sun against the facade. And it really does look like this from this angle. My boyfriend and I were there on vacation a month ago. And you would not be able to tell the difference between now and 1929 when this was painted. Well, he's not really my boyfriend, not after that. Speaking of sharp contrasts and bright lights. Can you believe from this angle, standing exactly there, that this pig had the audacity to reveal that he has been sleeping with one of my girlfriends?

I mean, can you imagine something like that? I mean, just because he's a young gorgeous broker with money oozing out of every pore, that gives him the right to sleep with my entire apartment and reveal it to me at such a sensitive artistic moment. Now every time I look at this painting that's all I can think. Me crying among those rocks, he driving away, and then that intolerable bus ride. Let's,...let's just move on. Shall we?

(*Lights rise on George Bellow's "Tennis at Newport."*)

"Tennis at Newport," George Bellows, 1919. I should have gone there. My sister invited me. I figured Maine with the hunk would be more calming. Notice in the painting the major emphasis is not on the tennis players in the foreground but on the spectators. See the avid tennis fans cruising around the lawn in their gowns and parasols? See them actually mesmerized more by other spectators? Much more interested in who's wearing what and whom on their arm then who's serving the insignificant ball? Believe me, it is just like that today. George Bellows was correct in 1919, and if he attended with my sister, her corporate climber of a husband, and their two angelic brats, with another on the way, the same crap's happening. It really makes me sick. And the money! And the food! What the hell do they care, they're all married, the plump little pigs. The whole scene is so repulsive, so republican. Let's just move on, come on, let's go. Oh God, I have such a migraine starting. By the way, the setting is the Newport Casino in Rhode Island. Come on, keep up!

(*Lights rise on Pierre Bonnard's "The Terrace at Vernonnet."*)

This is "The Terrace at Vernonnet," by Pierre Bonnard. Does it look like anyone influenced Pierre? Yes, Gauguin! Particularly the idea that things should be represented symbolically with intense patterns and colors. Also see the influence of Renoir's Impressionism and Pointillism which combined form a brand new term: "Intimist." And intimate this is. The lonely woman waiting. Like I was last Saturday night. The set table, the lone bottle of wine. I actually drank half of it at this point. As I wait for our landlord whom we invited to dinner. He's a nice guy. But he's kind of a bookworm. We are so behind in the rent, 4 months, we didn't know what else to do. Also pictured are two other women, one behind me, always helping, like my roommate Marissa. Marissa is a stewardess, gave up acting. And on the extreme right of the canvas, Ashley, my other roommate and recent fornicator with my ex brokerage beau. There she is arriving, as always, late. Apologizing with another personal crisis in her life, as always, brought on by her extreme beauty and lack of all moral certitude. In the center, the poor woman staring forward like a sacrificial lamb, that's me, knowing my two roommates would leave cause he'd like me. That was a terrible night. But at least we're all even with one month's credit on the rent. By the way, this was painted in 1920 and reworked in 1939. Oh God, how I suddenly hate this painting too.

(**WOMAN** *puts head in hands and breaks down sobbing.*)

Ahhhhhh! Oh God, what is happening in my life?

(**SHE** *sobs. Pause. Then still emotionally crazed, SHE signals everyone onward to follow HER as SHE exits.*)

Let's go. Come on. Keep up. Everyone keep up! EVERYONE ONWARD!

(**WOMAN** *exits. Blackout.*)

PRODUCTION NOTE

This works very well with an empty white frame upon one easel placed stage left, & another placed stage right. Remember, imagining these painting is always funnier than seeing them.

Breaking up the monologue: Another idea is to break up this monologue and have it serve as a thread throughout the play. It would play 2 or 3 times in the first act and two or 3 times in the second.

Starting the show with many in the cast as a tour group is fun too. And at the end of the show the group has grown to many.

If you are using projections instead of the blank canvas, images prior to 1923 as of this year (2007), are in the public domain. It moves ever year. 1924 for 2008 etc.. So the tour guide will have to refer to off left, off right or to the 4th wall (the audience) for images after that date. The 4th wall works well since she is talking right to us.

COSTUME

Offbeat, artistic.

Exhibits at the Metropolitan Museum of Art in New York
that corresponds to the scene:
MISGUIDED TOUR

Pablo Picasso
"The Blind Man's Meal" 1903

Georgia O'Keeffe
"Black Abstraction" 1927

Pablo Picasso
"Gertrude Stein" 1906

Lucian Freud
"Naked Man, Back View" 1992

Edward Hopper
"The Lighthouse At Two Lights" 1929

George Bellows
"Tennis at Newport" 1919

Pierre Bonnard
"The Terrace at Vernonnet" 1939

(All are mentioned in scene.)
See website: *www.LuigiJannuzzi.com*
for pictures and links.

FRAMED

Note: Based on the painting MEZZETIN, by Jean Antoine Watteau, French 1684-1721, European Paintings, The Metropolitan Museum of Art, New York. It is the painting of an actor playing the guitar in front of a theatrical backdrop. MEZZETIN is a character in the improvisational Italian theatre called Commedia dell'arte.

FRAMED won the best one act presented in The Midtown International Theatre Festival out of 40+ plays.

FRAMED was first produced by The Peddie Players at The Peddie School in Hightstown, NJ in July 2005. The play was directed by Michael Gallagher; produced by Robert Rund; set design by John Lucs; lighting design by Marilyn Anker; Crew and Advisors: Lynn Schreffler, Robert Gargiullo & Roby McClellan. The cast was as follows:

PAT...Dennis Jaybendy

VOICE ....Tom Stevenson

It was presented by the Metropolitan Theatre Company at New Jersey Repertory Company, Long Branch, NJ in July 2005. The play was directed by Luigi Jannuzzi; Executive producer Gabor Barabas; Artistic Director Suzanne Barabas. The cast was as follows:

PAT...Ben Masur

VOICE ....Marc Geller

It was produced by The Metropolitan Theatre Company in New York City as a selection of The Midtown International Theatre Festival, at the Workshop Theatre Main Stage, 312 West 36th St, 4th Floor, on July 2007. Executive Producer John Chatterton; Managing Director Emileena Pedigo; Artistic Director Glory Sims Bowen; Marketing Director Bob Ost. The play was directed by Elizabeth Rothan; Assistant directed by Lauren Embrey; produced by Luigi Jannuzzi/Elizabeth Rothan; lighting design by Alan Kanevsky; projection by Eric Christopher Hoelle. The cast was as follows:

PAT...Bruce Edward Barton

VOICE ....Jaron Farnham

(*Lights rise an actor sitting on a stool within a picture frame holding a guitar.*)

VOICE. Pat?

PAT. Yes?

VOICE. Do you know where you are?

PAT. Yes.

VOICE. Where are you?

PAT. I'm in a painting.

VOICE. And what are you doing in the painting?

PAT. Sitting on a stage.

VOICE. Good.

PAT. In a theatre.

VOICE. And what do you see?

PAT. An audience.

VOICE. Do they like you?

PAT. They don't know what to think.

VOICE. Are you afraid?

PAT. Well I,...I don't have any lines, there's no plot, they're,... they're not waiting for anything to happen. I think it's going to turn ugly soon.

VOICE. So you feel anxious?

PAT. Yea.

VOICE. Upset?

PAT. A little. How am I going to keep them interested? They're going to start leaving.

VOICE. Why don't you tell them you're an actor?

PAT. They know that.

VOICE. Why don't you tell them, they're not really there?

PAT. Because they think they are.

VOICE. Tell them.

PAT. Shhh.

VOICE. Go on.

PAT. I have their attention. Let me just sit here for a minute with it.

VOICE. Pat, tell them what you want to tell them.

PAT. I guess I should.

VOICE. This is your big moment.

PAT. Okay.

(PAT *puts down guitar, stands, to audience.*)

Welcome. I'm glad you're all here tonight. I'm an actor,...in a painting. You're an audience,...in a painting. If you were an actual audience, then... I wouldn't be able to see you. I think that's right, isn't it?

VOICE. You're in charge.

PAT. I think that's right. So we're kind of stuck here, in here together.

VOICE. Great logic.

PAT. And you can't leave cause I,...I need everyone here. Well you can't leave anyway cause you're in this with me. I think that's right, isn't it?

VOICE. Ask about the artist.

PAT. I'll get to it.

VOICE. Suppose they leave?

PAT. I just covered that, they can't.

VOICE. Why not?

PAT. It's a painting. You can't leave a painting.

VOICE. I'm pretty sure I see someone walking out.

PAT. That's part of the painting, they can't actually walk out.

They're just always in that process of walking, kind of
like everyone else is always listening.

(*To audience.*)

Where was I?

VOICE. Ask about the artist.

PAT. Oh. (*To audience.*) Uh,...do any of you know the artist?
I want to ask about the painting. And I'd like to know
which of you did it. (*Pause.*) Now don't kid me. I know
who the kidders are.

(*Pointing to audience member.*)

I know you're a kidder. (*Pause.*) And you. (*Laughs.*)

VOICE. Pat, if one of them is the artist then it may be only
the portrait of the artist, not the artist.

PAT. Oh no.

VOICE. See, that's your problem.

PAT. And what would the portrait know.

VOICE. As much as you.

PAT. So what should I do?

VOICE. Well, maybe you're not a painting.

PAT. I'm supposed to be a painting.

VOICE. My point is, maybe you're not.

PAT. Then what am I?

VOICE. Maybe you're an actor in a painting.

PAT. That's what I am.

VOICE. My point is maybe you shouldn't be looking for a
painter, you should be looking for a playwright. Maybe
you're in a play.

PAT. Well I do have lines.

VOICE. Paintings have lines?

PAT. Well, no.

VOICE. Paintings have characterization?

PAT. Hmmm.

VOICE. Paintings have humor?

PAT. In a way.

VOICE. They tell a story?

PAT. Well that's what I want to find out, what is my character, what are my lines, what's my story?

VOICE. So you don't think you have any of those?

PAT. No. I don't know what the hell I'm doing. Actors are
supposed to know what the hell's going on. Right?

VOICE. Not always.

PAT. You don't just like,...stand here.

VOICE. Unless it's one of those "Theatre of the Absurd"
pieces.

PAT. But paintings just stand there.

VOICE. Yea.

PAT. That's why I'm pretty sure I'm a painting.

VOICE. Makes sense.

PAT. And audiences in paintings are the only type of audiences that would put up with this crap.

VOICE. No, you'd be amazed what audiences will put up
with.

PAT. So based on the lack of all theatrical common sense, if
you will, I'd have to assume,. . .I'm in a painting.

VOICE. Yet I've noticed some in the audience are moving.

PAT. Some are fidgeting, reading their programs, cough-
ing, so it's upsetting and I don't understand that but.

VOICE. Pat, my point is,...it does seem theatrical on some level.

PAT. (*Pause.*) Wait a second, who are you?

VOICE. Another good point, Pat.

PAT. And you're not in the painting.

VOICE. True, paintings rarely have soundtracks.

PAT. And you tend to know what's going on.

VOICE. I have my questions.

PAT. Are you the painter?

VOICE. No.

PAT. Are you the playwright?

VOICE. No.

PAT. Do you know either?

VOICE. No. But Pat, I do have something really frightening to tell you.

PAT. What?

VOICE. This is the last page.

PAT. You have a script?

VOICE. Yea, but this is the last page so if you have any more questions ask them quickly.

PAT. Well uh...

VOICE. Very quickly, half a page left.

PAT. Well, I'd like to know where I came from, why I'm here and where am I going. I'd like to know who you are.

VOICE. The next line reads: "I don't know."

PAT. Is there a name on the script, a telephone number?

VOICE. On the front?

PAT. Anywhere.

VOICE. No. Nine lines left.

PAT. But what happens then?

VOICE. We can start over.

PAT. But what happens to us?

VOICE. It says "lights begin to fade on actor in frame". So I guess that answers something.

(*Lights begin to fade.*)

PAT. You don't think the playwright's going to write more lines for us, give us a plot, meaning, do you?

VOICE. I think the artist's gone, Pat. And we're at the last line.

PAT. (*Pause.*) What is it?

VOICE. (Pause.) Well, that was the last line, Pat. (*Pause.*) But there's an author's note.

PAT. Read it.

VOICE. Author's note: Remember,...as an actor in a painting, you only have to play the one moment that the audience is frozen with you.

PAT. Okay.

VOICE. Contrast this to a real play where you'd have to play many moments, hours full.

PAT. That's true.

VOICE. So I would suggest you smile, look appealing, perhaps on the verge of doing something, like playing your guitar. And for this one moment, and that's all you need, you will be the envy of every actor having the audience captivated with you,...and in you,... forever.

PAT. (*Pause.*) Oh,...I never thought of that.

VOICE. It's a lot easier than most actors have it.

PAT. Yea,...I like that.

VOICE. You have your audience. They have you.

PAT. Sure.

VOICE. Now it says the lights fade more. So smile.

PAT. Smiling.

(**ACTOR** *picks up guitar.*)

VOICE. You pick up your guitar.

PAT. Picked it up.

VOICE. You're about to play.

PAT. About to play.

VOICE. Sitting in your frame.

PAT. Yup.

VOICE. The audience is riveted.

PAT. I like this. This is a perfect part for an actor.

VOICE. Lights fading.

PAT. Let's do this again sometime.

VOICE. Fading.

PAT. And I really feel like I'm having a moment.

VOICE. Fading.

PAT. Even though it is,...forever.

(*Blackout.*)

COSTUME

Simple or close to what the actor is wearing in the painting.

PROPS

A guitar, a stool, and if you choose, a large frame.

Exhibits at the Metropolitan Museum of Art in New York
that corresponds to the scene:

FRAMED

Jean Antoine Watteau
"Mezzetin" 1719

*(This painting was used on the cover of the 1994 guide to The Metropolitan Museum of Art.)

(This painting is the scene.)

Also by LUIGI JANNUZZI...

The Appointment

The Barbarians Are Coming

A Bench at the Edge

For the Love of Juliet

Night of the Foolish Moon

With or Without You

DATE DUE

			PRINTED IN U.S.A.

SAMUEL FRENCH STAFF

Nate Collins
President

Ken Dingledine
Director of Operations,
Vice President

Bruce Lazarus
Executive Director,
General Counsel

Rita Maté
Director of Finance

ACCOUNTING
Lori Thimsen | Director of Licensing Compliance
Nehal Kumar | Senior Accounting Associate
Josephine Messina | Accounts Payable
Helena Mezzina | Royalty Administration
Joe Garner | Royalty Administration
Jessica Zheng | Accounts Receivable
Andy Lian | Accounts Receivable
Zoe Qiu | Accounts Receivable
Charlie Sou | Accounting Associate
Joann Mannello | Orders Administrator

BUSINESS AFFAIRS
Lysna Marzani | Director of Business Affairs
Kathryn McCumber | Business Administrator

CUSTOMER SERVICE AND LICENSING
Brad Lohrenz | Director of Licensing Development
Fred Schnitzer | Business Development Manager
Laura Lindson | Licensing Services Manager
Kim Rogers | Professional Licensing Associate
Matthew Akers | Amateur Licensing Associate
Ashley Byrne | Amateur Licensing Associate
Glenn Halcomb | Amateur Licensing Associate
Derek Hassler | Amateur Licensing Associate
Jennifer Carter | Amateur Licensing Associate
Kelly McCready | Amateur Licensing Associate
Annette Storckman | Amateur Licensing Associate
Chris Lonstrup | Outgoing Information Specialist

EDITORIAL AND PUBLICATIONS
Amy Rose Marsh | Literary Manager
Ben Coleman | Editorial Associate
Gene Sweeney | Graphic Designer
David Geer | Publications Supervisor
Charlyn Brea | Publications Associate
Tyler Mullen | Publications Associate

MARKETING
Abbie Van Nostrand | Director of Corporate
  Communications
Ryan Pointer | Marketing Manager
Courtney Kochuba | Marketing Associate

OPERATIONS
Joe Ferreira | Product Development Manager
Casey McLain | Operations Supervisor
Danielle Heckman | Office Coordinator, Reception

SAMUEL FRENCH BOOKSHOP (LOS ANGELES)
Joyce Mehess | Bookstore Manager
Cory DeLair | Bookstore Buyer
Jennifer Palumbo | Customer Service Associate
Sonya Wallace | Bookstore Associate
Tim Coultas | Bookstore Associate
Monté Patterson | Bookstore Associate
Robin Hushbeck | Bookstore Associate
Alfred Contreras | Shipping & Receiving

LONDON OFFICE
Felicity Barks | Rights & Contracts Associate
Steve Blacker | Bookshop Associate
David Bray | Customer Services Associate
Zena Choi | Professional Licensing Associate
Robert Cooke | Assistant Buyer
Stephanie Dawson | Amateur Licensing Associate
Simon Ellison | Retail Sales Manager
Jason Felix | Royalty Administration
Susan Griffiths | Amateur Licensing Associate
Robert Hamilton | Amateur Licensing Associate
Lucy Hume | Publications Manager
Nasir Khan | Management Accountant
Simon Magniti | Royalty Administration
Louise Mappley | Amateur Licensing Associate
James Nicolau | Despatch Associate
Martin Phillips | Librarian
Zubayed Rahman | Despatch Associate
Steve Sanderson | Royalty Administration Supervisor
Douglas Schatz | Acting Executive Director
Roger Sheppard | I.T. Manager
Geoffrey Skinner | Company Accountant
Peter Smith | Amateur Licensing Associate
Garry Spratley | Customer Service Manager
David Webster | UK Operations Director